Dragon Unbound

Also From Donna Grant

Don't miss these other spellbinding novels!

Dragon King Series
Dragon Revealed
Dragon Mine

Reaper Series
Dark Alpha's Claim
Dark Alpha's Embrace
Dark Alpha's Demand
Dark Alpha's Lover
Tall Dark Deadly Alpha Bundle
Dark Alpha's Night
Dark Alpha's Hunger
Dark Alpha's Awakening
Dark Alpha's Redemption
Dark Alpha's Temptation
Dark Alpha's Caress
Dark Alpha's Obsession
Dark Alpha's Need
Dark Alpha's Silent Night
Dark Alpha's Passion

Dark King Series
Dark Heat (3 novella compilation)
Darkest Flame
Fire Rising
Burning Desire
Hot Blooded
Night's Blaze
Soul Scorched
Dragon King (novella)
Passion Ignites
Smoldering Hunger
Smoke And Fire
Dragon Fever (novella)
Firestorm

Blaze
Dragon Burn (novella)
Heat
Torched
Dragon Night (novella)
Dragonfire
Dragon Claimed (novella)
Ignite
Fever
Dragon Lost (novella)
Flame
Inferno
Whisky and Wishes (novella)
Heart of Gold (novella)
Of Fire and Flame (novella)
A Dragon's Tale (novella compilation)

Kindred Series
Everkin
Eversong
Everwylde
Everbound
Evernight
Everspell

Dark Warrior Series
Midnight's Master
Midnight's Lover
Midnight's Seduction
Midnight's Warrior
Midnight's Kiss
Midnight's Captive
Midnight's Temptation
Midnight's Promise
Midnight's Surrender (novella)

Dark Sword Series
Dangerous Highlander
Forbidden Highlander

Wicked Highlander
Untamed Highlander
Shadow Highlander
Darkest Highlander

Rogues of Scotland Series
The Craving
The Hunger
The Tempted
The Seduced

Chiasson Series
Wild Fever
Wild Dream
Wild Need
Wild Flame
Wild Rapture

LaRue Series
Moon Kissed
Moon Thrall
Moon Bound
Moon Struck

Shield Series
A Dark Guardian
A Kind of Magic
A Dark Seduction
A Forbidden Temptation
A Warrior's Heart

Druids Glen Series
Highland Mist
Highland Nights
Highland Dawn
Highland Fires
Highland Magic
Mystic Trinity (connected)

Dragon Unbound

A Dragon Kings Novella

By Donna Grant

1001 DARK NIGHTS

PRESS

Dragon Unbound
A Dragon Kings Novella
By Donna Grant

1001 Dark Nights
Copyright 2022 Donna Grant
ISBN: 978-1-951812-84-3

Foreword: Copyright 2014 M. J. Rose

Published by 1001 Dark Nights Press, an imprint of Evil Eye Concepts, Incorporated

Sign up for the 1001 Dark Nights Newsletter
and be entered to win a Tiffany Key necklace.

There's a contest every month!

Go to www.1001DarkNights.com to subscribe.

**As a bonus, all subscribers can download
FIVE FREE exclusive books!**

Acknowledgments from the Author

I want to thank everyone at 1001 Dark Nights Press for another amazing release. Being a part of this publishing family is a truly wonderful experience. I love each and every one of you. Liz, MJ, and Jillian—three extraordinary women I'm proud to know and call friends.

A special thanks to Charity Hendry, Chelle Olson, and Teresa K. for the many emails, texts, and phone calls—and patience. The Dark World is huge (and growing), and I wouldn't be able to keep it straight without all of you.

Last, but not least, to *you*. Thank you for buying and reviewing my books. I wouldn't be here now without you. Thank you for taking this incredible journey with me and the Dragon Kings. We've seen a lot, but there is *so much more* coming.

One Thousand and One Dark Nights

Once upon a time, in the future…

*I was a student fascinated with stories and learning.
I studied philosophy, poetry, history, the occult, and
the art and science of love and magic. I had a vast
library at my father's home and collected thousands
of volumes of fantastic tales.*

*I learned all about ancient races and bygone
times. About myths and legends and dreams of all
people through the millennium. And the more I read
the stronger my imagination grew until I discovered
that I was able to travel into the stories... to actually
become part of them.*

*I wish I could say that I listened to my teacher
and respected my gift, as I ought to have. If I had, I
would not be telling you this tale now.
But I was foolhardy and confused, showing off
with bravery.*

*One afternoon, curious about the myth of the
Arabian Nights, I traveled back to ancient Persia to
see for myself if it was true that every day Shahryar
(Persian: شهريار, "king") married a new virgin, and then
sent yesterday's wife to be beheaded. It was written
and I had read that by the time he met Scheherazade,
the vizier's daughter, he'd killed one thousand
women.*

Something went wrong with my efforts. I arrived in the midst of the story and somehow exchanged places with Scheherazade — a phenomena that had never occurred before and that still to this day, I cannot explain.

Now I am trapped in that ancient past. I have taken on Scheherazade's life and the only way I can protect myself and stay alive is to do what she did to protect herself and stay alive.

Every night the King calls for me and listens as I spin tales. And when the evening ends and dawn breaks, I stop at a point that leaves him breathless and yearning for more. And so the King spares my life for one more day, so that he might hear the rest of my dark tale.

As soon as I finish a story... I begin a new one... like the one that you, dear reader, have before you now.

Chapter One

The scream tore through her head, jerking her awake immediately. Her gut clenched with dread as fear pooled in her belly. Before she could fully register the first one, a second scream filled her mind, the echo making her clutch her head as her lungs seized.

Not again.

Tamlyn didn't hesitate to jump to her feet and make her way through the winding hallways until she burst outside. She tripped, caught herself, and ran as fast as she could, letting her connection guide her up the canyon wall and across the field to Ferdon Woods.

The killings have to stop.

Tamlyn wasn't sure that day would ever come, but she couldn't think about that now. She had to focus all her energy on the connection. A sound above caused her to glance up. For just a second, she thought it was a dragon, though dragons never crossed onto their land. She tripped and stumbled again but managed to right herself before she went down. She didn't dare look up again. If a dragon found her, so be it. She had more important matters to worry about tonight.

Her lungs burned as she pumped her arms and legs, forcing herself to keep going when all she wanted to do was collapse. Time wasn't on her side. It never was, but there was a particular urgency in the scream that night. She didn't allow herself to think what would happen if she didn't get there in time.

The forest was just ahead. She knew Ferdon Woods all too well. It would hide her approach, but it held many dangers—some traps and…other things she would rather not think about.

Yet, she didn't have time to go around. If she was going to succeed, then she had to go *through* the woods. She pursed her lips and continued. The quarter moon offered little light. Not that Tamlyn needed it. She had used this path so many times she could walk it blindfolded.

At the last moment, she diverted her course. Something within urged her to use a different route, even as a rational part of her warned that it was suicide to walk through the brush.

Once inside the forest, the thick canopy of trees refused to permit any light to slip through their foliage. Tamlyn halted, her breaths harsh as her lungs sought to fill with air. Her gaze scanned the area with trepidation for the things that lurked in the night.

The trees were massive. Not just in height but also girth. Her gaze swung to the right. Dense growth that hid most of the gnarled tree roots covered the ground. One wrong step would be all it would take for her to find herself wounded...or worse. A look to the left gave her a glimpse of the road. It was likely safer, but not by much. Especially if someone were waiting for her. Forward was more of the same impenetrable brush.

Tamlyn swallowed and squared her shoulders as she started forward. She wanted to run through the woods. Instead, she would have to carefully pick and choose her path. Her boots gave her traction to keep from sliding over the roots. Twice, her ankle rolled, but her boots were thick and sturdy, keeping her from becoming severely injured.

Her palm scraped against the bark of a tree when she reached out to right herself. She kept her attention on where she placed her feet, but she made sure to look around often. It would be foolish to forget what lived within the forest.

She jumped when she heard a sound to her right. Tamlyn froze, listening. After several tense minutes, she spotted the wings of an owl flying away. She hated that she had to traipse through these woods, hated what forced her to put herself in danger time and again. She couldn't let herself linger on those thoughts, though. She had tried to ignore the call, attempted to ignore who she was.

That hadn't turned out so well. She still carried that guilt, and she probably always would. She had to be in these woods just as the owl had to hunt. It was her destiny, no matter how much she wished otherwise.

The longer it took her to get through the forest, the more anxious she became. Time wasn't on her side. Just as she was about to throw caution to the wind, she heard it. The whisper. Tamlyn hurried to the next tree and hunkered down as she tried to determine which direction it had come from. Her lips flattened when she heard two human males talking. She had to lean to the side to find them, but then she spotted the soldiers hidden near the main path through the forest. Was this what her intuition had warned her about? It wasn't normal for anyone to be out in the woods, especially not soldiers.

They didn't know who she was, but that didn't matter. They knew they were after someone who'd escaped the city. That meant they would capture anyone they saw and sort out the details later. Bastards. Every damn one of them.

The snap of a twig behind her made her heart jump into her throat. She heard the heavy breathing. Tamlyn began to shake. Every fiber of her being told her to turn and see where the beast was so she could get away. The breathing was a dead giveaway that it was a brineling. The four-legged beasts were twice the height of a human, covered with thick, green skin, and had two curved horns jutting from their foreheads. The animals were huge, but they moved with a speed that defied their size.

If the brineling had seen her, it would've already attacked. Her only hope was to not draw its attention. If she avoided that, she might survive the night. It took all her willpower to remain still when she wanted to run and hide. Sweat dripped from her forehead and into her eye. She blinked against the sting, but she didn't move.

The beast's breathing grew slower, deeper. It sounded as if it were right on top of her.

Her attention had been on the men. A mistake since there were more dangerous things in the forest than the soldiers. The ground trembled slightly beneath her at the brineling's approach. The bush beside her rubbed against her neck, making it itch.

Tamlyn bit back a yelp at how close the brineling was. She could've reached out and touched it. She didn't know how it had missed her, and she didn't care. Only once before had she seen a brineling, but that had been from a distance. And she didn't dare tilt her head back to get a better look at the creature when it was this close.

Its breathing suddenly hushed as it lowered itself, readying for attack. Tense seconds stretched on for an eternity as the animal grew still and quiet. Then it leapt forward with a roar. The great horned creature rarely lost its prey, and it had its sights set on the two soldiers.

At its roar, the men screamed and turned to attack with spears and swords. Tamlyn started running at the sound of their bellows of pain amid the brineling's noises. She prayed her feet found solid ground as she put distance between herself and the hungry animal. Limbs ripped at her face and body as she ran, and roots fought to trip her, but she kept upright. The last thing she wanted was a brineling on her tail. She'd never outrun it.

One minute, she was racing through the forest. The next, she was flat on her face. She gasped, pain radiating through her body at the air having been knocked out of her. Even that didn't stop her. She pushed herself up and started running again.

When her lungs finally unseized and she was able to take a full breath again, she felt lightheaded. Tamlyn had to force herself to slow to a walk. If soldiers had been stationed that far into the woods, there could be more.

She was nearly out of the forest. As much as that pleased her, it didn't mean that things would be easier. Because she was looking, she found two more soldiers hiding near the road. They were intent on the brineling. That was likely the only reason they hadn't heard her barging through the forest so recklessly. Tamlyn skirted them and hurried from the woods. She sighed in relief at the same time a chill ran down her spine. She was leaving one lethal environment for another.

Tall, stone gates with soldiers stationed along the battlements stood before her. Beyond the gate was the city of Stonemore and the Tunris Mountains. The city had been built into the tallest peak of the mountain range, rising from the ground to the very top where the ruler of Stonemore lived and reigned. The mountains on either side of the city curved inward. And that, along with the wall, created an impenetrable fortress.

Tamlyn had been in the city far more than she wanted to admit, but she knew very little about it, other than where to sneak in and out, and what level the temple was on. Stonemore looked pretty in the night with the moonlight reflecting off its reddish stones. Except she knew what kind of wickedness lived within the thick walls.

She remained close to the woods and ignored the closed gates. Another hundred yards, and she glanced up to make sure the soldiers weren't looking her way, then dashed across the empty expanse and right to the storm drain. Tamlyn plastered her back against the wall and listened to hear if anyone raised an alarm at spotting her. When all remained quiet, she gripped the lock and pulled. The metal came undone easily in her hand. Every time she took this route, she was surprised that no one had checked the storm drains or the locks. She lifted the heavy metal grate overhead so she could slip inside. Her muscles screamed in protest when she slowly lowered the cover back into place so it didn't bang. She turned to look around the four-foot, arched drain.

Tamlyn's breathing was loud even over the tinkling of water that rushed past her feet in the drain. She ignored her wet feet and crouched, walking until she reached the other side of the drain without a grate. She paused at the entrance and peeked around the corner, first one way and then the other. When she didn't see anyone, she eased out and straightened, careful to remain in the shadows.

This was the part she hated the most. It was almost too easy to get into the city. Getting out was another matter. She shoved aside those thoughts and turned right, walking close to the wall. She made it up the first level and then the second without incident. The third was trickier because there was more housing than shops, which meant more people. She managed to dodge soldiers and residents alike to get to the fourth level.

Once there, she stared at her destination—the temple, its beauty marred by the horrors committed within. Memories tried to surface, but Tamlyn shoved them aside. The past was the past, and it needed to remain there.

It took forever for her to reach the temple since there were more soldiers on this level. Thankfully, their attention was on other things. When she made it, she still had to get across the wide square in front of it. All she could do was hope that her timing was right when she pushed away from the wall and walked across the open expanse.

She ducked out of sight when she rounded the left side of the temple. Tamlyn braced her hands on her knees and drew in deep breaths. That was the worst part of her mission. Every time, she feared she would be stopped and questioned.

Once she had composed herself, she stood. Tamlyn ignored the doors. Instead, she looked up at the windows. The one she needed was the highest of them all. The climb was perilous, the stones worn nearly smooth. But someone had once climbed the temple because there were footholds or handholds that couldn't be seen unless you were scaling the wall. She always wondered if the person had made it out. She liked to believe they had.

Tamlyn had made this climb before, so she knew exactly where to go to get to the window quickly. She took a deep breath and sent up a silent prayer that the soldiers on the battlements didn't look her way. If they did, she would be spotted easily. She reached up and got a good hold of the edge of a stone before putting the toe of her boot on another and hoisting herself up.

It had been a life-or-death situation that'd brought her to this side of the temple years ago. She'd never imagined she would return time and again, but here she was once more. Would she make it out this time? She didn't want to think about what might happen to her if she got caught.

Her muscles screamed in protest as she made her way up. Every time she did this, she swore it would be the last. It was a lie she told herself to get through each event because she would continue this journey until they finally killed her.

Finally, her hand gripped the windowsill. She slowly pulled herself up to look through the glass window. She saw the boy sitting on the floor, his frightened gaze locked on the door. Tamlyn was shocked at his age. Normally, the children she came for were much younger. The boy had to be seven or eight. There was no way she could carry him like she had the others.

Her mind raced to find a way to get him out. No matter how hard she racked her brain, she couldn't come up with anything. She either had to leave him to his Fate or take him as she did the others and leave things up to chance.

She looked at his face. Tears fell down his cheeks. He knew what was to happen. His terror was palpable. There was no way she could leave without him. Her course had been set the instant she heard the scream in her head earlier.

Tamlyn made sure her footing was solid before lifting one hand from the sill and tapping her finger on the glass. His head snapped to her, but he didn't move. She was fast losing her strength. She couldn't stay in this position much longer. Tamlyn motioned him to her. Still, he hesitated. She tried once more. Her arms were shaking, her fingers beginning to go numb. She was about to lose her grip. If he didn't come now, they would both die tonight.

To her relief, he jumped up, rushed to the window, and opened it. She pushed up and sat on the windowsill to give her arms and legs a rest. Then she looked at him.

"Who are you?" he asked, his blue eyes wide with fear.

"Tamlyn. I'm here to help you."

He glanced at the door. "No one can help me."

"I climbed this wall for you. We can go down together, or you can stay here and see how things turn out."

He shook his head before she finished. "I don't want to stay. But..."

"I know," she said softly. "It's scary. There's a chance we won't make it. But it's a choice you alone can make."

He lifted his chin, his slim shoulders squaring. "I'll do it."

"Good lad," she said with a wink. "I'm going to get into place. I need you to climb out and onto my back. Be sure to close the window."

He glanced down and then nodded jerkily.

"You can do this," Tamlyn told him.

That seemed to bolster him. She flexed her fingers and hoped she would be able to maintain her grip with his added weight. Tamlyn held onto the sill and dropped down, using her arms to hold her until she got both her footholds.

"All right. Come on," she urged.

The boy climbed out and scooted to the edge of the sill on one side of her. He closed the window behind him.

"Good," she said with a nod. "Now, get onto my back. Use my body however you need to, but make sure you have a good hold on me. Just be careful not to choke me."

The instant he told her that he was in place, she began climbing down. She hadn't gotten very far when she realized that she would never be able to hold them both. Her fingers were slipping, and her arms were shaking so badly she could barely move them.

And then she lost her grip.

Air rushed past them as they plummeted to the passageway below. Just before they hit, they jerked to a stop. Somehow, they hung suspended in midair for a heartbeat before falling the last few feet. The impact jarred her, but nothing like what *could've* happened.

She sat and turned to the boy. "Was that you?"

He shrugged. "Maybe."

"Thank you." She jumped to her feet. "Come on. We've got to get out of the city."

Those at Stonemore didn't know who was rescuing the children, but each time she came to the city, there was something else that hadn't been there before. This time it was the soldiers in the forest. What would be next? They would catch her eventually. Until then, she would save as many as she could.

She took the boy's hand and turned to retrace her steps. The only way out was to go down, and that meant walking across the empty square again. She kept a tight hold of the boy while also making sure their steps were easy and casual. One of the nearby soldiers turned to look at them. He started toward them, but another soldier told him to forget them. No doubt those two would be in trouble shortly, but she couldn't let her thoughts linger on that. By her reckoning, everyone who didn't stop the sacrifices was complicit.

Once they were off the fourth level, it took no time before they neared the drain. Tamlyn kept watch as she nudged the boy inside. When she knew that no one was coming, she ducked in after him. Then she lifted the grate on the other end and slipped out.

The boy looked at the forest. His face was pale, but he didn't shrink away. He knew what was at stake, just as she had that long ago night when *she* escaped. It was either die in the temple or take a chance in the forest. Tamlyn hadn't had to think twice about it.

"We're going to be moving fast," she told him. "Keep a hold of my hand. No matter what, stay with me. When I stop, you stop. When I go, you go. Don't look back, and don't hesitate. And don't make a sound."

He met her gaze and nodded.

She held out her hand. When he placed his in hers, she ran toward the woods.

Tamlyn wanted to use the easy path, but the soldiers were there. She was forced to retrace her steps from earlier. The thought of the brineling made her hesitate a bit, but she didn't have another option. They moved slower since the boy jumped at every sound. Eventually, he blocked out the night sounds and focused on her.

Every step got her closer to freedom. She was hypervigilant. That's what allowed her to spot the brineling. She didn't know if it was the same one from earlier or not. The safe thing to do would be to stay put and wait for it to walk away. She was about to tell the boy that when the toll of alarm bells sounded from Stonemore.

Shit. They knew the boy was gone. She couldn't see the city from the woods, but she didn't need to in order to know that they were rallying the army. They would track her and the boy. Hiding from a few soldiers in the forest was one thing. Being tracked by them was another.

The boy's breathing grew erratic as he looked back at the city. She touched her finger to her lips as she looked at him. The brineling might just save them. If it wasn't there, they would be cornered quickly enough, but the beast would be drawn to the noise of the soldiers.

Already, the beast's head turned in the direction of Stonemore. Tamlyn heard the clang of weapons as the soldiers rushed into the forest. She watched the brineling, waiting to see when it would attack. The warriors had fanned out, but there wasn't enough of them to cover the entire woods. She'd head to the left if she thought she could get away, but her best chance was to go straight through.

When the brineling crouched, she tightened her hand on the boy's. "Get ready," she whispered.

The soldiers walked slowly through the forest, thrusting their swords into bushes in case someone was hiding. Animals scattered from them and their noise. The brineling had gone still as stone. It waited for them to get closer. Tamlyn spotted soldiers coming near. She wanted to bolt, but she knew that timing was everything.

When the brineling leapt to attack, she jumped and pulled the boy with her. The soldiers' shouts joined the creature's bellows as the men rushed to help their comrades. Tamlyn didn't look back. She ran, half dragging, half pulling the boy with her. Their only chance was making it out of the forest.

Chapter Two

The air swept over Cullen, wrapping him in an embrace. He closed his eyes and soared through the night sky, basking in the silence and freedom. It was as if everything he'd hoped for had come to fruition.

He opened his eyes and looked at the ground far below him. He had left behind the fertile, flat, green fields and flew over rugged mountains dotted with waterfalls. Trees rose to the sky amid the jagged mountain slopes. He focused his gaze farther ahead. With his enhanced senses, he could see far into the distance to the canyon. It looked as if someone had split open the ground. He flapped his wings, flying faster in his eagerness. There was something about the canyon he couldn't get enough of.

Cullen had arrived on Zora five weeks earlier at Constantine's bidding. It had been time for a new adventure—though Cullen wasn't thrilled there was a new foe. But enemies came from every direction when you were as powerful of a creature as a Dragon King. Many times, evil tried to tip the scales in its favor. That's when Cullen and the rest of the Dragon Kings made an appearance.

From the moment everyone at Dreagan learned that the link between Earth and Zora was open, the Kings had wanted to go and get a glimpse of their dragons again. It had been entirely too long since they had laid eyes on their kin. Yet, Cullen and most of the others had to remain behind on Earth, chomping at the bit to see Zora.

Just when Cullen thought he might never get to see his Garnets again, they'd gotten word from Con, King of Dragon Kings, that all unmated Kings were needed. Cullen had been the first through the Fae doorway connecting the two realms. The moment he stepped into Zora and saw the dragons, emotion overwhelmed him. It lodged in his throat, choking him, but at the same time, the steel vise around his chest loosened for the first time in eons. He could've watched the dragons for eternity.

Con and Rhi's twin children, Brandr and Eurwen, ruled Zora at Cairnkeep. That's where the Dragon Kings congregated to get up to speed on things. Cairnkeep was the base in Zora—much as Dreagan was on Earth. Except the twins hadn't built a grand manor as the Kings had. But Cullen suspected that would come soon enough.

He had been shocked to discover humans in Zora. It seemed that anywhere the dragons went, mortals weren't far behind. Brandr and Eurwen hadn't wanted to make the same mistakes the Kings had on Earth, so they'd set up sections on the realm for humans with an invisible barrier that kept them out of the dragons' territory.

It had worked. Or they *thought* it had. Recently, however, the twins had learned that some humans had been capturing and torturing dragons for their magic. Cullen had missed out on aiding in punishing the mortals responsible. At least those poor dragons had been freed, and the mortals responsible dealt with.

But it wasn't just humans on the realm. There were those with magic and others, like Jeyra, who aged at a much slower rate. Even before Jeyra mated a Dragon King, she had helped by sharing information about her city and those who ruled it. Despite that, some unknown foe had begun attacking and killing dragons. It was why Con had called for the Kings.

Cullen reached the beginning of the canyon. From his vantage point from above, it looked like the smallest crack that had splintered then became a gaping hole. No part of Zora wasn't beautiful and unspoiled. It reminded him of Earth before the humans arrived. But he didn't want to think about that. Not here, not in this pristine place that wasn't buzzing with planes, trains, cars, satellites, or mortals.

He hadn't realized how tense he'd been on Earth until he arrived in Zora. The Kings couldn't give up their home. Not only did their presence keep the realm safe, but their home was near where magic welled from the planet. It was why they had chosen that spot for Dreagan.

Still...Cullen would have a difficult time leaving Zora. Even with humans.

Each Dragon King had been given a quadrant to keep watch over to see if anyone could catch the new enemy. He'd made it his mission to know every inch of the land he had been sent to. He flew over it several times a day. For five weeks, he and the other Kings had waited for an attack or some sign of their adversary. But there had been nothing.

He alternated when he made his passes in hopes of seeing something. The sky was a soft gray now. Bright light was beginning to show over the horizon, announcing that dawn was fast approaching. This was Cullen's favorite time of day. He loved seeing the sunlight chase away the darkness and bathe the world in its radiance. But, most of all, he loved being able to fly freely. It wasn't something any of the Dragon Kings had been able to do in eons, not since they sent the dragons away and hid from the mortals.

His heart was both joyful and wrenched at the same time. The fact that these dragons were the descendants of those on Earth brought a smile to his face. Just as it did knowing they were safe and free to live as they were supposed to.

On the other hand, his gut churned with bitterness and regret that the Kings had once had a world like Zora, but things had gone badly, leaving them only one choice. Sadness weighed heavily upon him at what he and the other Kings had lost. Their world might not have been perfect, but it was as close as it could be in his eyes. Earth was a place where he had to search to find beauty. Something that had once been everywhere before the humans cut down forests, drained lakes, moved rivers, and blasted mountains, all to cover it with concrete and build shopping malls or houses. How much longer could it continue before they depleted Earth of all her resources? What would the tedious, wrathful mortals do then?

Cullen's thoughts skidded to a halt when he caught sight of a dark-haired woman bursting from the forest on the human side of the barrier with a small boy with black hair. They were running, the woman looking over her shoulder often. Cullen suspected the duo was coming for dragon territory, and since humans weren't supposed to cross over, it meant that he had to stop them.

Just as he dipped his wing to turn around and confront the pair, a group of armored and uniformed men poured from the forest. Many had some form of injury—blood covering nearly all of them. Cullen wasn't sure whose blood it was, but it didn't matter. The men were after the woman and child. No human was supposed to come onto dragon land, but he wasn't going to stand by and watch the men attack defenseless people.

Cullen tucked his wings and dove from the sky. As he neared, he opened his mouth and released his power of fog. It poured from him, falling to the ground and slowly spreading. He glanced at the woman and lad to see them near the edge of the barrier. His attention returned to the men. He curled into a ball as he shifted, calling his clothes and weapons to him as he landed on his feet.

Slowly, he lifted his head and grinned. He could see clearly through the fog, but the soldiers couldn't. They were disoriented and trying to discern where it had come from. Cullen remained still and, with a simple thought, dispersed the fog enough for the men to see him.

"Who the bloody hell are you?" one of the soldiers demanded.

Cullen let his gaze move over the group as he held his axe in his left hand and his sword in his right. "You have one chance to turn around and leave."

"Get out of our way," another ordered.

Cullen shrugged. "So be it."

He tossed the axe, watching it imbed itself in one of the soldier's skulls. He then ducked a swing from a sword, only to pivot and lift his blade to stop another attack. He spun, slicing his sword through the abdomen of two men, who grabbed their stomachs and shouted with pain as they fell to the ground.

Movement next to him caught his eye. He glanced over to see the woman fighting alongside him with a staff. He didn't see the boy, and all he could hope was that the lad was safe.

Cullen had been fine fighting the group of soldiers on his own, but with the woman there, he knew it was only a matter of time before she got injured. She had skill, but she wielded a staff against blades. Which meant that he had to end this now. He could shift and douse them with dragon fire, which would mean instant death.

Or he could stop playing around and take them out.

He opted for the latter option because he wanted information from the woman, and he wasn't sure he would get that if she knew he was a Dragon King. Cullen moved quickly, pivoting, turning, lunging, and jumping until only a handful of the men remained. They quickly ran back into the forest and disappeared.

"You shouldn't have let them go. They'll be back with reinforcements," the woman said as she turned on her heel and started running to the canyon.

Cullen hadn't gotten a chance to talk to her so he followed. To his surprise, she didn't go through the barrier. Instead, she went down one of the sloped green walls to the canyon below. They reached the bottom, and she lengthened her stride. He couldn't be sure if she was headed toward the barrier or to the large tree in front of them.

His gaze followed the spiderweb of exposed roots that protruded from the crack running down the canyon wall. That's when he spotted the arched double doors. They were off their hinges, the roots slowly crumbling the doors into ruin. The woman didn't slow as she turned sideways and slipped between the narrow opening of the giant doors. Cullen quickly followed.

Inside, he came to a halt as he gazed in wonder. This wasn't a cave at all. It was an entrance of some kind.

His enhanced eyesight allowed him to see that the entry was large enough for four men to easily stand side by side. The smooth, perfectly rectangular stones seemed to almost glow. He thought it was magic, but a closer look told him that it was just the way the stone was. He spotted several staves leaning near the entrance, including the one she had used. She must have stopped here before coming to aid him in the fight. He looked ahead to find the woman descending some steps. He followed her down the well-worn stairs that had been expertly carved from the mountain stone and into another room.

A beam of light filtered down from above. He tilted back his head and realized that the light was coming from the top of the cliff several hundred feet above. Water dripped from tree roots that intersected in a strikingly complex system, only to drop into a large pool in the center of the room. His gaze slowly lowered as he looked about the chamber. He counted six—no, seven—different stairways, and numerous doors. But it was the four giant heads carved out of the canyon that captured his attention. It reminded him of the ancient statues in Cambodia.

They faced north, east, south, and west. North and south had their eyes open, while east and west had their eyes closed with small smiles on their lips. It was impossible to determine if the faces were male or female, but the artwork was so beautiful, he couldn't look away.

The sound of running feet finally pulled his gaze away. Cullen looked over to see the lad come from the shadows and throw himself at the woman. For the first time, he got a good look at her. To say she was lovely didn't do her justice. She was…exquisite.

Her dark skin had a golden-bronze glow to it. Her riot of black curls was tied at her nape with a leather string, the length hanging to her mid-back. She had an oval face with a stubborn chin and wide, full lips. Dark brows arched delicately over large, hazel eyes that held his. She was average height, her body toned. She wore brown pants that appeared supple and conformed to her legs. A dark green shirt of the same material laced up the front and covered her arms, hanging to her hips. A wide, brown leather belt accentuated her waist. He spotted the dagger against her leg, the top of the scabbard hooked to her belt, and the bottom strapped to her thigh.

The lad had a death grip around her hips as he stared at him with terror.

Cullen dropped to his haunches and smiled at the boy. "You needn't fear me, lad. Those men willna harm you."

"Don't make that promise."

At the sound of her voice, Cullen's gaze jerked to her face. The sweet sound was both sexy and commanding. And it caused something inside him to shift. Her voice had a slight lilt. Had they been on Earth, he would've asked if she hailed from somewhere in Europe.

Cullen slowly straightened. "I doona make promises I can no' keep. Who were those men?"

"Soldiers from Stonemore," she answered, her gaze never wavering.

"And why were they chasing the two of you?"

Her hazel gaze slid away. "That's none of your concern. You need to leave."

"My name is Cullen. I can help."

Her gaze returned to his. Just as her lips parted, another woman came out of a doorway to their left. She was statuesque and athletic. As she moved closer, Cullen realized that she was at least six feet tall. She wore an armored breastplate, a leather skirt cut into strips that fell past her knees, and greaves over her shins. He saw the hilt of a sword peeking over her right shoulder and strapped to her back. Her skin was pale, her blond hair plaited to fall down her back. But her dark eyes boring into him told Cullen that she didn't want him there.

"Tamlyn, who is this?" the blonde asked. "And why the hell is he here?"

Chapter Three

Tamlyn didn't understand why her heart still hammered as if she were in battle. And she couldn't stop looking at Cullen. She should've stopped him from following her into the ruins. She still didn't understand why she hadn't. No doubt, Jenefer and Sian would both demand an answer. Tamlyn hoped she had one by then.

She fisted her hands that still vibrated from the blows she'd received. No amount of training with a wooden staff prepared anyone for battle. She swallowed at Jenefer's question, all the while staring at the man before her. He had blond hair shaved on the sides and pulled away from his face on top. His beard was darker in color, but instead of hiding his jaw, it brought more attention to it. His bottom lip was fuller than the top, and his watchful, pale brown eyes missed nothing.

He wore a shirt the likes of which she had never seen before. The thin, dark gray material had short sleeves and molded to his thick arms and broad shoulders and chest, showing every muscle ridge. She caught sight of what looked like a dragon inked on his left arm, but the pattern got lost beneath his sleeve. His blue pants were made of some thick material that didn't look comfortable, and on his feet were heavy boots unlike any she had ever seen.

"His name is Cullen."

He bowed his head to Jenefer. "And you are?" he asked.

His voice caused Tamlyn's stomach to feel as if bees had taken up residence. How could someone's voice do that? As handsome as he was, she couldn't trust him. No matter that he had helped them.

Jenefer took a menacing step toward him. "Showing you the way out."

"I want to know why those men were after Tamlyn and the lad," Cullen said.

Tamlyn could tell that Jenefer was about to cause trouble. So, she hurried and said, "It was a misunderstanding."

Cullen's gaze slid to her. "A misunderstanding? A group of soldiers after a woman and a boy? Soldiers, who, I might add, you warned would get reinforcements and return. Try again."

"It's none of your damn business," Jenefer stated.

"I'm trying to help," Cullen said.

Jenefer crossed her arms over her chest. "Help somewhere else."

Tamlyn pulled away from the boy and put her hand on Jenefer's arm. She knew her friend was trying to protect them, but Tamlyn didn't want the man harmed. He *had* helped. If it weren't for his arrival, they never would've made it to the ruins. "Will you take the boy and get him some food? He needs to rest. I'll handle this."

Cullen and Jenefer stared at each other for a long moment before Jenefer sighed loudly and dropped her arms to her sides. "Fine."

Tamlyn smiled and nodded to the boy, indicating that he could go with Jenefer. Once the two were out of sight, she turned to Cullen. "Thank you for the help, but you shouldn't have gotten involved."

"They almost caught you."

"I know." It had been close. Too close. Closer than she liked to admit. "The best thing for you is to leave and forget about us."

"And if I don't?"

It was her turn to sigh. "If you come back, we'll be gone. Now that you know of this place, it isn't safe for us."

"Because you believe I'll tell someone."

She flattened her lips and gave him a knowing look. "Everyone has a price."

"No' me."

"I owe you a debt for slowing the men. I'll find a way to repay you, but you need to go."

Cullen stood his ground. "You can repay me by telling me what happened."

"If you wait, you'll encounter the soldiers again. I won't come out to help you this time. Neither will Jenefer."

Was it her imagination, or did he smile?

"Then you better hurry and tell me," he pressed.

Tamlyn rolled her eyes in irritation. Cullen seemed like a man she could trust, but it could be a ruse. Yet, she didn't think so. He would've had to know exactly where she would head, and she had been very careful. No one knew about their sanctuary.

Well, no one but him now.

If he were with the army from Stonemore, nothing she told him would be news. It wasn't as if she would lower her guard and allow him close. That might be something a spy from Stonemore would try, but as she'd already told Cullen, they would move. It didn't matter that he knew where she was now or what her story was.

"I saved the boy from death."

Cullen's brows drew together. "How?"

"He was to be sacrificed."

Righteous anger clouded his pale brown eyes. "Why would anyone want to kill a child?"

"He has magic."

Cullen shrugged. "So?"

Now it was her turn to frown. Only those with magic were nonchalant about the mention of it. Even then, many who had magic pretended they didn't. There wasn't a person on the realm who didn't know why a human with magic was a problem.

She took a step back and thought about the fog that had suddenly rolled in as she ran from the soldiers. Cullen had appeared within the fog. Maybe she'd been too quick to open up. "Who are you?"

"I told you."

Tamlyn shook her head and took another step back. "Everyone knows why magic is an issue. You don't. Why?"

"You doona have to be frightened of me."

"I'm not so certain."

His chest rose as he drew in a deep breath and slowly released it. "I'm new to the realm."

That drew her up short. "New? How?"

"It's…a long story."

"Only infants arrive here. Not adults."

His lips flattened. "As I said, it's a long story."

"One I want to hear."

"Finish yours first. Why would anyone want to sacrifice a child?"

She put her hand to her forehead and shook her head. Was it possible that he didn't know? He could've come up with another story if he lied. Only an idiot would claim ignorance—unless he really didn't know.

"Tamlyn. Please," he asked softly.

She dropped her arm to her side. "The humans on this realm are in two groups. Those with magic, and those without. Those without have persecuted and hunted those with any type of ability almost from day one. When the infants are found, no one can tell if they have magic or not. It's up to those who take the child in to tell their leaders. Once they're notified, the children are imprisoned and killed. These people discovered that if you kill those with magic early on, few can stand against you later on."

"Bloody hell," Cullen said as he ran a hand down his face. He shook his head, his gaze on the ground. "These children have no idea they are no' supposed to use magic."

"No."

"And when they do, it seals their Fate."

"Yes."

Cullen lifted his head and looked at her. "These people must be stopped."

"That's what I'm trying to do, but there are too many of them."

"How do you learn when a child will be killed? Do you have a source in the city?"

Tamlyn swallowed nervously. "Not exactly."

"Tell me. I'm no' your enemy."

For some reason, her lips parted, and the words fell from her mouth without hesitation. "I'm a Banshee. I hear the screams of the children about to die."

A muscle ticked in his jaw. "What of the other cities?"

"I don't know how everything works."

"But there's a possibility other children are being killed?"

She nodded, her gut twisting as it did each time she thought about this. "Those without magic are terrified of us."

"Why? Have you attacked them?"

"I'm sure some have. But for years, all we've tried to do is stay alive. They don't just kill the children. If they find one of us, they kill us."

His brow furrowed deeply. "How do they know they're killing someone with magic?"

"I don't think they care. If there's even a hint of it spoken about someone, they take action."

"It's like the witch trials," Cullen mumbled as he paced.

Tamlyn wanted to ask what the witch trials were, but she decided to wait. "Those with magic hide. It's our only option."

"Perilously close to dragon land," he pointed out.

She twisted her lips. The entrance was close to the barrier, but a large part of the underground city was beneath the dragons' land. She would rather have them to worry about than her kind. The dragons hadn't hunted her. Not that she wanted to test that theory.

"I told you that you shouldn't get involved."

He halted and looked at her. "I wouldna be able to look at myself in a mirror if I didna do something."

"What can you possibly do?"

His lips tilted in a cocky smile. "More than you know."

"You have magic?"

"Aye."

"What kind?"

"You saw some of it," he told her. "The fog."

Her eyes widened. "Tell me how you came to be on this realm. And is there a way for me and my friends to leave it?"

"You wouldna be hunted in my world for having magic, but I doona think my world would be better."

"That's because you haven't lived here your entire life," she snapped.

"True."

She briefly closed her eyes, hating when she lost her temper.

"Are there other Banshees?" Cullen asked.

Tamlyn nodded. "A Banshee found me. That's how I learned what I was. She hid me and ran after a couple of days because men were on her trail. I've not seen her since."

"Are you telling me that you were one of those children about to be sacrificed?" he asked after going very still.

"Yes," she replied softly.

They stared at each other for several seconds in silence. Then she asked, "Why are you on this realm?"

"I'm helping my friends, who have been attacked by an unknown foe."

"And you got here how?"

He hesitated as if he didn't want to tell her. "A doorway."

His answer floored her. "What kind of magic was used?"

"Fae."

"Fae?" she asked in shock. "That can't be. The Fae are a myth."

He lifted one shoulder in a shrug. "Afraid no'."

"Are you Fae?"

"No. I have several good friends who are, but I'm no' a Fae."

She caught and held his gaze. "What are you, then?"

"I'm no' sure you want to know."

"I do."

He wrinkled his nose. "I doubt that."

"I told you what you wanted to know. It's only fair that you do the same."

Cullen licked his lips. "I'm a Dragon King."

Chapter Four

Cullen wasn't sure what to make of Tamlyn's silence as she stared blankly at him. The seconds stretched until he shifted uncomfortably. Maybe he'd been wrong in thinking he could tell her the truth.

"Tamlyn?" he asked hesitantly.

Her throat bobbed as she swallowed. "D–did you say Dragon King?"

Cullen inwardly winced. That was panic in her voice. "Aye." When she didn't say more, he tried another approach. "You doona have to be afraid."

"I disagree," she said after a bark of laughter. "The one thing everyone knows is to fear dragons, but most especially those like you."

That got his attention. As far as he knew, Eurwen and Brandr had gone to great lengths to have minimal contact with humans, if any at all. "How do you know about Dragon Kings?"

She shrugged. "Everyone knows such things. I guess I was taught them, just as I learned about the sun and the sky."

"And what were you taught about us?" Cullen couldn't explain the resentment or the indignation he felt. But it was there, simmering within him.

"That you're the enemy. That if we encounter a Dragon King, it will end in our death."

Cullen tamped down his anger. Barely. How could the humans think such things about them when they'd had no interaction? It was ridiculous. "You were taught wrong."

"I don't think so. The dragons keep us out for a reason."

"Aye. And they have a good one."

She snorted, her apprehension giving way to irritation. "I doubt that."

"I suppose you doona want my help now that you know who I really am."

"That's exactly it."

He shot her an incredulous look. "You'd rather take your chances with the soldiers than me?"

She crossed her arms over her chest and lifted her chin. "Yes."

"I didna take you for a fool."

"You don't know me," she retorted.

That he didn't, but he was trying to help. Cullen opened his mouth to speak when a brunette woman rushed from one of the darkened doorways. She came to a halt as she looked between them. Cullen noted her petite stature and slim build. Unlike Tamlyn and Jenefer, this woman wore a long, tan frock, the lower skirt wrapping around her. The neck was simple, showing little in the way of skin. He couldn't tell if the sleeves were long or if they were hidden by the thick leather gloves pulled up to her elbows. Over her upper body was a short apron made of the same leather as her gloves, stopping just below her hips. Various belts, buckles, and bags were attached to the apron.

Her wavy, brunette hair was haphazardly pulled away from her face with a lock dangling over her eyes. The rest hung down her back. Pale green eyes watched him with fascination.

"Tamlyn," the woman said as she started to her friend. "Jenefer said we had company."

Tamlyn nodded. "He's leaving."

Cullen ignored Tamlyn and smiled at the new arrival. "My name is Cullen. I helped Tamlyn and the lad. I'm offering more assistance, but she's refused."

"I'm Sian," the woman said with a bright smile. "Thank you for aiding Tamlyn. We didn't know she'd left."

"I didn't have time to wake either of you."

Sian shot her a dark look. "One of these days, you're going to get yourself into a fix. How are we to help if we don't know? Now," Sian said as she returned her attention to Cullen, not giving Tamlyn time to reply, "I need all the details about how you met Tamlyn and what happened."

"No," Tamlyn said as she stepped between them, her face directed at Sian.

Cullen blew out a breath. "I'd be happy to tell you, but I'm afraid

Tamlyn is nervous about me being here."

Sian stepped to Tamlyn's side to see Cullen, her brow furrowing. She looked between him and Tamlyn before sliding her gaze back to him. "Why is she scared?"

"Because I told her I was a Dragon King."

Sian's face visibly paled.

Cullen shook his head and threw up his hands. "Tell me, have either of you seen a Dragon King harming anyone?"

"That doesn't matter," Tamlyn said.

At the same time, Sian replied, "No."

Cullen caught Tamlyn's gaze. "If you think I'm going to sit by and allow children to be murdered, you're wrong. None of my brethren will. We *will* do something."

"Dragons don't cross the barrier," Sian said.

Bloody hell. Cullen had forgotten about that. "Then I willna shift. I'll stay in this form. No humans need ever know."

"Neither the dragons nor those who rule them care what's happening to us." Tamlyn shrugged as if stating such a fact was all that was needed.

Cullen released a sigh. He didn't know Eurwen or Brandr well—hell, he didn't know them at all—but he couldn't imagine the twins allowing such a travesty if they could do something about it. "I might have recently arrived on this realm, but I willna sit idly by and do nothing."

"Even if it means starting a war?"

His head jerked to the right at the sound of Jenefer's voice. She stood on one of the stairs above him, one foot on the step below, cocking her body sideways. "War?" he asked.

"Humans and dragons are to remain separate. That's why there's a barricade. Erected by dragons," Jenefer explained, speaking as if he were an imbecile.

Cullen clenched his teeth. He wanted to help, but it was apparent they didn't want it. And it wasn't as if he could force them to accept his aid. He turned to Tamlyn. "If you change your mind, let me know."

Tamlyn didn't reply. Jenefer glared. Sian had her hands clasped behind her back, but she moved her right hand and gave him a little wave and a tentative smile. At least she didn't hate him. Cullen turned and started the long trek of steps to the outside. Everything within him told him to stay, but he couldn't. There was too much contention. Even if Tamlyn had agreed, Jenefer wouldn't have made things easy.

Cullen felt their eyes on him as he squeezed through the door. He paused, wondering if he should stay regardless. The ruins belowground looked immense, and there would probably be another exit. His gaze looked to the side through the invisible wall to the quadrant he was supposed to guard. He might want to stay and help, but he couldn't. Not yet, at least.

He was irritated and angry. Physical activity was just what he needed to burn off some of it. Cullen chose the steepest part of the cliff and began to climb. He could've jumped to the top without much thought, but the exertion would be better.

When he reached the summit, sweat covered him, and his breathing was labored. Yet, he still looked for a fight. He glanced toward the forest, half hoping soldiers would appear so he could take his fury out on them. Unfortunately, his wish didn't come true. They had returned to pick up their dead, however.

Cullen glanced down the canyon. The doorway was hidden, but he knew it was there. He pivoted and walked through the barrier to dragon land. How odd that he had just been thinking about how great it was not to have any humans around on Zora. He'd been ecstatic that Brandr and Eurwen had ensured the mortals kept to their parcels of land instead of encroaching as the humans had done on Earth.

Now, all he could think about was a Banshee who risked her life to save children from being sacrificed.

"*Cullen?*"

He sighed as he came to a halt at the sound of Con's voice in his head. Dragons spoke through a mental link. "*Aye. I'm all right.*"

"*What happened?*"

"*I've discovered something you, Brandr, and Eurwen should know.*"

There was a beat of silence. "*We'll be right there.*"

The link disconnected. Cullen ran a hand down his face. As much as he resented the humans for their part in the dragons having to be sent away, he couldn't stop thinking about the bairns. Those children were defenseless. How could anyone do such a thing to them?

Cullen shifted to his true form and spread his wings. He jumped into the air and flew to the top of the mountain. It was his favorite place. He had a beautiful view of the area he guarded. It would also be a good spot to await the others. His gaze slid to the canyon, but he didn't let it linger.

It wasn't long before he spotted his friends in the distance. Cullen returned to human form, calling his clothes to him once more. He was surprised to see Vaughn instead of his mate, Eurwen. The three Kings landed and shifted in quick succession.

"Please tell me you saw the evil," Brandr said, his gaze penetrating.

Cullen looked into Constantine's black eyes and then at Rhi's son. "No' the foe you're wanting, no."

"What happened?" Con asked.

Cullen looked between father and son. Both had black eyes, but Con had short, wavy, blond hair while Brandr had long, black hair like his mother's. "It was quiet as it has been. I was doing patrol at dawn. That's when I saw the woman and child racing from the forest," he explained and pointed to the woods.

"I take it someone was after them," Vaughn replied.

Cullen met his Persian-blue eyes and nodded once. "About a dozen armored men."

Brandr didn't bat an eye. "We doona meddle in the affairs of humans."

"I wasna going to allow a woman and a bairn to be run down and killed," Cullen stated.

Con glanced at Brandr before turning his attention on Cullen. "I take that to mean you intervened."

"Aye. I used my power and covered the area with fog to give the lad and woman a chance to escape."

"That better have been all you did," Brandr warned.

Cullen slowly turned his head to him. The urge to punch him was high, but he was a guest on Zora. This wasn't Earth. Cullen had to remember that. "As a matter of fact, it wasna. I fought them."

"Do you want to start a war?" Brandr bellowed, his black eyes flashing with fury.

Vaughn's anger was palpable when he asked Brandr, "And you condone the murder of a child and a defenseless woman?"

"We don't get involved," Brandr stated, his nostrils flaring. "They stay on their land, and we stay on ours. I doona give a shite what happens over there. I thought if anyone could understand the things Eurwen and I put into place, it would be the Kings. Now you want to make the same mistakes you did on Earth here. I willna let it happen. Zora willna be another Earth. The dragons willna lose another home."

Con calmly said, "That will never happen. I gave you my word, son."

"Good. Then take care of Cullen," Brandr ordered.

Cullen's hands fisted. "You—"

Con put a hand up to stop Cullen. Then he faced Brandr. "First, every Dragon King who is willing to risk their lives to fight your foe is dozens of millennia older than you. Second, we've been through more than you can possibly imagine, so I willna be *taking care* of anyone. The Dragon Kings know what to do."

A muscle ticked in Brandr's jaw.

"As for the woman and child, there's more to the story. Which Cullen would get to if you'd but listen," Con added.

Once Con looked his way, Cullen forced his fingers to loosen and release the tension in his body. But it wasn't easy. "The woman came out with a staff and held her own, but there were too many. I did enough to chase off the rest."

"You mean killed," Brandr added.

Vaughn crossed his arms over his chest and shot Brandr a dark look. Con kept his gaze on Cullen.

Cullen did his best to ignore Brandr and continued. "The woman then turned and ran. I thought she was headed to the barrier. Instead, she went down the canyon. I wanted to make sure the lad was safe, so I followed her through a hidden doorway. I found myself in underground ruins. I discovered the boy was safe, and she was the reason for it. She had risked her life to smuggle him out of Stonemore, where he was to be sacrificed."

"Bloody hell," Vaughn murmured as his arms dropped to his sides. "How did she find out about the sacrifice?"

Cullen hesitated. "It's her ability. She's a Banshee."

"A what?" Brandr asked, shock causing his features to slacken.

That got everyone's attention. Con's brows snapped together. "Are you serious?"

Cullen nodded. "Her name is Tamlyn. She told me that she hears the screams before a child with magic is about to die. She sneaks into Stonemore and escapes with the children. I doona know how many she has saved. She's no' alone, though. There are two other women with her. One was dressed like a warrior and nearly our height. The other was petite and wore peculiar clothing."

"What kind of clothing?" Brandr asked.

Cullen slid his gaze to him, noting the small frown. "Thick gloves up to her elbows."

"And an apron to her hips?"

"Aye. You know what she is?"

Brandr briefly closed his eyes. "An Alchemist."

"Shite," Vaughn said.

Cullen glanced at Con, who had yet to say anything. Con's gaze moved back to Brandr. "How do you know about the Alchemists?"

"They are highly prized among the humans. Some are treated very well so they will stay in the city and provide the wealthy with whatever needs they have," Brandr explained.

Vaughn's shoulders rose with his breath. "And the others?"

"There is talk that they're kept as slaves. Hidden away from those in the city."

Cullen squeezed the bridge of his nose with his thumb and forefinger. "Tamlyn said that a Banshee rescued her the night she was to be sacrificed. She went on to explain that those with magic are hunted by those in the city. When the gifted took a stand, the humans lost. Mortal families take in the infants that arrive here. The instant they show any kind of magical ability, the leaders of the city are alerted, and the child is killed."

"Kill them before they become strong," Con said, disgust lacing his words.

Brandr shook his head. "We can no' interfere. Everything Eurwen and I have put into place will be wiped away."

"I can go in this form. No one has to know I'm a Dragon King," Cullen suggested.

Vaughn nodded. "I'll go with him."

"And when you're attacked? What then?" Brandr demanded. "You'll use magic to fight them off?"

Cullen shrugged. "If it comes to that."

"No. You should have never crossed the shield to help." Brandr slashed his hand through the air. "All you're to do is look for our adversary."

Cullen stared at him for a moment. "And when all the humans with magic are killed? Who do you think the mortals will target next?"

"You really think they could take us on?" Brandr asked with a snort.

Con sighed softly. "They were no' stronger than us on Earth."

With a hiss of agitation, Brandr leapt off the mountain and shifted to fly back to Cairnkeep.

"Well, that went well," Cullen said into the silence that followed.

Vaughn shrugged. "It's bairns we're talking about. How can we sit back and let this happen?"

"Because this isna our realm," Con said. He held up a hand for quiet when Cullen tried to speak. "I agree with both of you, but you also need to understand where Brandr is coming from. If Eurwen had been here instead of taking care of other business, she would've agreed with her brother. They set up this system because of the failures we had on Earth. We sent our dragons away. Thankfully, they have this place, but I stand with my children when it comes to keeping Zora safe for the dragons."

Cullen's gaze moved to the canyon, Tamlyn's face filling his mind's eye. She was courageous and strong, but she had nearly been caught this time. How many more times would she succeed before she *was* caught? The thought left a sour taste in his mouth. He might not be from Zora, but he knew right from wrong. He wouldn't give up. He'd figure a way to continue on with his mission while also helping her.

Chapter Five

"Have you lost your mind?" Jenefer demanded angrily.

Tamlyn rolled her eyes as she broke a loaf of bread apart to dole it out to the seven children they were caring for. Jenefer had asked that same question the moment Cullen left the ruins. Tamlyn knew it wouldn't matter how she answered. Jenefer would keep asking because that was just her way.

"She didn't know who he was," Sian told Jenefer for the second time.

Jenefer made a sound at the back of her throat as she ladled soup into the children's bowls. "Well, we do now. We need to move."

"Really?" Sian asked, her face crestfallen. "I finally have a good lab."

Tamlyn straightened and smiled at the kids. Her gut churned every time she thought about leaving the ruins. She didn't want to go. It was a good place. It offered everything they needed with plenty of room to grow.

"Eat up." She motioned for her friends to follow her out of the room. "I don't want to talk about this in front of them."

"Why not?" Jenefer demanded. "They know the harsh truths of the world."

Tamlyn fought against a surge of anger. "That doesn't mean they need it thrown in their faces again and again. They're *children*. Let them have some portion of the lives they were supposed to."

"I agree," Sian said.

Jenefer rolled her eyes. "You always agree with Tam."

"Not true. I've sided with you on occasion," Sian said, her chin lifting.

Tamlyn sighed. "I believed Cullen. I think he wants to help. He was appalled by what I told him."

"He's a Dragon King," Jenefer replied as if that said it all.

A small smile pulled at Sian's lips. "He was cute. I loved his hair. Did you see the markings on his arm? I wonder what it was."

That only made Jenefer roll her eyes again.

Tamlyn tried not to think of just how handsome Cullen was—in a wild, intense way that she never expected to find appealing. But it certainly looked good on him. Very, *very* good.

Sian interrupted her thoughts when she said, "He was right. We haven't seen any Dragon Kings harm anyone. We've been told to fear them."

"With good reason. Don't be such a dolt. Dragons have more magic and power than any other being on this realm. I can't imagine what a Dragon King has," Jenefer said.

Tamlyn leaned back against one of the stone walls. "Neither of you saw the fog. It came out of nowhere. I believe he is who he says he is."

"All the more reason to get out of here now," Jenefer said.

Tamlyn looked at her. "Why? Because he might come back to help? He won't go to any humans."

"You would put those children's and Sian's life in danger because you want to trust a Dragon King?" Jenefer asked, pointing at Sian.

Sian shoved Jenefer's arm out of the way. "Hey. Don't put me in the middle," she said before hurrying away, a hurt expression on her face.

Jenefer winced, her lips parting as she rushed after her. "Sian. Shite. I'm sorry."

Tamlyn left them to it. No doubt Jenefer would be apologizing for quite some time. She loved her friends, but sometimes Jenefer couldn't see around the past. It defined her, as it had with all of them. Jenefer had saved her life. Tamlyn knew she wouldn't be alive now if it weren't for Jenefer.

And Sian... Tamlyn couldn't help but smile. Despite Sian's rough life, she still found things to smile about, still found ways to laugh. It was only because of her vivacity that Jenefer smiled at all. Sian was the one who kept their trio together.

Tamlyn turned the corner and watched the children eat. They weren't loud or boisterous as kids usually were. They were traumatized and distrustful of everything. Tamlyn had once been like that. So had Jenefer and Sian. They had pulled through it, though, and so would these youngsters. It was either that or go down a dark path.

Not that she would blame any of them if they did. For some, they had been taken from the only family they knew and readied to be sacrificed so those without magic didn't have to live in fear.

But others were abused in ways Tamlyn didn't want to even think about. It made her soul scream at the injustice of it all. These were defenseless children, who counted on others for help. Those people betrayed them in the worst ways possible.

Tamlyn's head turned in the direction of the corridor Jenefer had disappeared down. She knew her friend had been physically abused. Jenefer hated to be touched in any way—or she used to. All that had changed when they found Sian. Something about the Alchemist softened Jenefer's rough edges. Tamlyn had never thought anything would temper the Amazon, but Sian had done it with a single smile.

There were times Tamlyn envied the love the two had found with each other. Her jealousy never lasted long, though. Her friends deserved happiness. They all deserved to live somewhere they weren't hunted, imprisoned, or killed. It wasn't as if it were their fault they had magic. None of them had a choice in any of it.

More than once, Tamlyn had wondered why those with magic didn't come together and fight those without once and for all. Long ago, a small group had. They had won and created Highvale for all those with magic to come and live. It was set well away from any of the other settlements. It served its purpose, but it didn't answer the needs of so many others. Tamlyn and her friends weren't the only ones who had left Highvale.

They had tried to live in the city for a time, but the knowledge that others out there needed help drove them to leave. They had devoted their lives to helping others, and Tamlyn hoped they had done some good.

She took note of their food stores. They would need more soon. The sound of Jenefer's and Sian's voices made her think of the true reason the three of them had left Highvale—Sian's sister, Mair, who was still a slave.

Sian would never rest until her sister was free. Jenefer would never stop planning for how to liberate Mair. And Tamlyn would be right there with them. The plan was nearly finished.

Tamlyn once more thought about Cullen. With him on their side, they could free Mair easily. It would begin a war, and that wasn't something Tamlyn was sure she could live with. Yet, how could she think that when Mair suffered every day? Sian had told them about the cruel hand of their master. How he would beat them and fondle them. He was a scourge upon the realm. If anyone deserved to meet their Fate, it was him.

Tamlyn and the children finished cleaning up from the meal when Jenefer finally came back into the kitchen. The Amazon wore a smile, telling Tamlyn that she and Sian had made up.

"Don't give me that look," Jenefer said, but there was no heat to her words.

Tamlyn shrugged. "You hate when Sian is mad at you."

Jenefer sank onto one of the benches and dropped her head back with a sigh. "You have no idea how much. It's like a dagger in my gut."

"She knows you don't mean to hurt her."

"She said I hurt you."

Tamlyn sat on the opposite side of the table and looked into Jenefer's brown eyes. "I can hold my own."

"That's what I told her," Jenefer said with a smile. It faded as she licked her lips. "I've got a bad feeling, Tam. I've had it for a while now."

"What kind of feeling?"

Jenefer shrugged helplessly. "I've been trying to sort that out. I can't pinpoint it. I just know in my bones that something bad is coming."

"You mean Cullen's arrival."

"Yes. Maybe." She sighed loudly. "I don't know. I don't like that he knows about this place, and I really don't want him helping us."

Tamlyn raised her brows. "Think how easily we could get the children. I wouldn't have to climb that tower again."

"The lad told me you fell. I didn't share that with Sian, but she'll find out eventually," Jenefer warned.

Tamlyn glanced away. "He was heavier than the others."

"Which is why you shouldn't go alone. I can't believe you got in and out again."

Tamlyn cleared her throat and refused to look at Jenefer.

"Oh, no," the Amazon stated. "Spit it out. All of it."

Tamlyn put her arms on the table and messed with her short nails. She didn't look up as she told Jenefer about the soldiers awaiting her in the forest and the brineling. Only when she finished did she dare look up. The look of shock and anger on Jenefer's face told her that she was in for an argument.

"Have you lost your damned mind?" Jenefer asked softly.

Tamlyn shrugged. Jenefer had been asking her that a lot lately. Maybe she *had* lost her mind. "There wasn't time to wake you."

"There's always time. I swear, Tam, if you don't start taking me with you, I'm going to bolt the doors so you can't leave."

"No, please."

Jenefer leaned forward, her gaze intense. "Then you wake me," she said, punctuating each word.

Tamlyn nodded. "I promise."

"Good." Jenefer sat back. "Now, about moving."

"We aren't going anywhere."

Chapter Six

Time and again that day, Cullen's gaze found the canyon. It didn't matter if he was flying on patrol or sitting atop the mountain. His thoughts remained on Tamlyn and what she had told him. It was in his genes to help others. The right thing to do was to save the bairns. It didn't matter the arguments. Not when it came to animals and children, in his eyes.

The repercussions if he disregarded Con's order would be severe, and yet he had no other choice. To ignore the plight of innocents made him no better than those he fought against. He wouldn't be able to look at himself in the mirror if he didn't do something. The problem was that he didn't know the realm. He couldn't just walk into a human city and mingle as he did on Earth. Things were much different on Zora.

Then there was the peace—if you could call it that—between the dragons and humans. He could very well shatter that, causing the chaos that Brandr and Eurwen had gone to such lengths to ensure didn't happen.

He stretched his wings out from his perch atop the mountain and shook his head. When things got to be too much on Earth, the Dragon Kings found their mountains on Dreagan, sometimes sleeping for several centuries at a time. Other times, they used their mountains to shift and be in their true form away from the mortals' prying eyes. But on Zora, he could remain in dragon form for as long as he wanted.

The humans there knew about the dragons—and knew to stay off their land.

It had been the same on Earth once. Unfortunately, it hadn't lasted long. The Kings had lost so much. Eurwen and Brandr had changed tack.

It wasn't that they weren't making mistakes, they were making new ones. But that's how it went. Cullen didn't fault them for taking the actions they had, but he knew in his gut that continuing to let humans with magic suffer would come back to haunt them all.

A speck in the distance drew Cullen's attention. He zeroed in on it and soon realized it was two dragons. It wasn't much longer before he saw Vaughn's teal scales and Eurwen's peach scales and gold wings.

Cullen remained and waited for the couple to reach him. Eurwen was the first to land. The daughter of the King of Dragon Kings and a royal Light Fae, she had distinctive scales that set her apart from the others— just as her brother did. She nodded to Cullen as she shifted into human form. Vaughn took his human shape as he landed beside his mate. They joined hands immediately. Vaughn's blue eyes swung to him.

Cullen shifted and eyed his visitors. "What brings you two here?"

"I want to hear your story again," Eurwen said.

She had Rhi's silver eyes and Con's blond waves, a direct contrast to her twin's dark coloring. Cullen hadn't spent much time with either of them, but he had come to realize that Brandr was the quick-tempered one while Eurwen considered her options.

Cullen didn't expect a different outcome after Con and Brandr's visit earlier, but he detailed his encounter with Tamlyn for Vaughn's mate. When he finished, Eurwen's face was lined with concern.

"I think we should do something," Cullen finished.

Eurwen said nothing as she walked a few steps away and put her back to them. She wrapped her arms around herself as the wind whipped her long, blue skirts against her legs. Her long, blond locks danced in the breeze, but she didn't seem to notice.

Cullen slid his gaze to Vaughn. "What is she doing?"

"Thinking," he replied.

Cullen didn't believe there was much of a chance for Eurwen to agree with him. Yet, she hadn't made a swift decision as her brother had. That said something. At least she was considering all sides.

Vaughn looked over his shoulder to the green canyon, but he said nothing. Cullen wanted to ask what his friend was thinking. In the end, he decided to wait until Eurwen had a chance to speak her mind. Though Brandr had decided instantly, Cullen wasn't fooled by his cavalier attitude. Everyone was disturbed by the fact that children were being harmed.

Finally, Eurwen turned around. Her lips were pinched with stress, and her forehead wrinkled with a frown. "I wish things were simple.

Things aren't black and white, despite what they might appear to be."

"I understand. Brandr made his position clear," Cullen told her. "Just as Con did."

Eurwen's silver eyes watched him. "You disagree?"

"They're bairns. I doona care what species they are, they're innocent."

She rubbed her temple as her gaze lowered. "That's why I wanted to hear your encounter from your lips."

"And?" Cullen pushed.

Eurwen shook her head helplessly as she glanced at Vaughn. "Each way I look at this, it destroys everything Brandr and I have built."

"It doesna have to," Cullen stated.

Vaughn's brows snapped together. "What do you mean?"

"No one knows me. I can go to Stonemore and find the children."

Eurwen slashed her hand through the air. "No, you can't. It isn't as if they're all held together. The kids are with different families. It isn't until they show magic that the families alert the authorities."

Cullen shrugged. "Then I'll wait."

"How are you to know when the kids are taken?" Vaughn asked. "Then there is the fact that you know nothing about these humans' customs."

"I'll find out. Jeyra can tell me a lot," Cullen said.

But Eurwen shook her head. "Jeyra's people are different from those at Stonemore. Every human city here is vastly different. They might be on the same landmass, but they'd be as different as Americans are from Europeans, as they are from Asians, and so on. If the kids were being harmed in Jeyra's home city of Orgate, I'd agree with you."

"Then I'll talk to Tamlyn." Cullen wouldn't give up. There was a way, and he would find it eventually.

Vaughn's lips pressed into a flat line. "You said she wouldna help."

"I'll convince her."

Eurwen said, "You won't. She understands why we shouldn't get involved. There's a delicate balance here. It took some time for Brandr and I to get it this way. To disrupt that would send everything into chaos."

Cullen glanced to his left where he spotted dragons in the distance. He didn't want to alter the dragons' lives. They deserved a peaceful place to live after everything their ancestors had gone through on Earth. "I agree."

"Good," Eurwen said.

Cullen's gaze slid to her. "I would sooner cut off my own arm than do anything to harm what the dragons have here. But I can no' call myself a King and stand by without helping innocents."

"Cullen, wait," Vaughn said.

He cut his eyes to Vaughn, silencing him instantly. "I knew there were humans here with magic, and I understood that they didna live with those without. But I wasna aware of them being hunted or harmed." He turned back to Eurwen. "Were you?"

Her silence was answer enough.

"Eurwen," Vaughn said, his brow furrowed deeply.

They could speak later. Cullen still needed answers. "How do you know?"

Eurwen hesitated before blowing out a breath as if defeated. "There have been times Brandr and I walked among the humans. We wanted them far away from us and the dragons, but we needed to make sure they understood how dangerous it was to go near the barricade that separated our two cultures."

"I'd have done the same," Vaughn replied.

Cullen glanced at his friend before asking Eurwen, "Then you know Stonemore?"

She nodded woodenly. "Unfortunately. That city is one of the oldest and grandest of all the metropolises, but the people there are unforgiving. Orgate accepted those who lived longer like Jeyra and used them as warriors. Had she been in Stonemore, they would've killed her."

"Jeyra doesna have magic," Vaughn said. "She simply ages differently."

"Stonemorians see those with any kind of special ability—like unnatural aging—as the enemy."

Cullen tucked that information away. "Did you tell the people to fear dragons?"

She thought about that a moment. "We warned those in leadership positions to make sure their people didn't cross the threshold into our domain. We let them know harm would come to them."

"Did you tell them to fear Dragon Kings?"

Her frown deepened. "We never said anything about Dragon Kings."

"Someone had to," Vaughn said. "Jeyra knew about them. It's why she sought out the crone to pull one to the realm to be punished."

Eurwen threw up her hands. "We wanted the humans to know that it was better for everyone if they stuck to their land. Did we want them to fear crossing the barrier? Absolutely. But we never said anything about Dragon Kings. Why would we? We ruled here, not any of you."

"You're a Dragon Queen. Brandr is a King," Vaughn added.

Cullen scrubbed a hand over his chin. "Tamlyn and her friends showed real terror when I told them who I was. Tamlyn told me she was taught from an early age to fear all dragons, but especially Dragon Kings."

"I don't know where the humans are getting that information," Eurwen said.

Vaughn twisted his lips. "I think we need to find out."

Cullen looked between them. "I have to help the children."

"I'm not sure there's a way to do that and not start a war," Vaughn said.

Eurwen swallowed as she shrugged. "There isn't."

"We're dragons. With magic," Cullen reminded them. "We can do it."

Vaughn eyed Eurwen, surprise in his voice when he asked, "You're seriously considering it?"

"He's right," she said and jerked her thumb to Cullen. "It's one thing for cities to ban those with magic. It's something else entirely to kill them. I'm ashamed to say that I didn't care what the humans did to each other. But when helpless children are involved, I can't pretend any longer."

Cullen didn't celebrate her statement. Though he was delighted to have someone on his side, he knew things wouldn't be easy. "Con and Brandr are going to be livid."

"Which is why there can't be anything to disrupt the balance here," Eurwen told him. "Nothing. The minute there is, you return. I want your word, or I won't help."

Vaughn visibly winced. "Honey, hold up a moment. I told you my concerns because I thought you might agree with my sentiment."

"Obviously, I do," she retorted. She quirked a brow. "You knew there was a chance I would go against Brandr."

Cullen understood what Vaughn was getting at. "Brandr has adjusted his thinking to allow some Kings onto Zora to help battle this new enemy, though it goes against everything both of you agreed on."

"Eons ago," Eurwen added.

"The point is," Cullen said with a meaningful look, "Brandr will only be able to bend so far before he breaks."

Eurwen walked to Vaughn and put one arm around him as she laid her other hand on his chest and looked into his eyes. After a long moment, she turned her head to Cullen. "I know you think Brandr unsympathetic and emotionless, but we've had to be. He has a hard shell to guard a sensitive heart that wants to protect everyone and everything. I thought up most of the rules we put in place. I mellowed through the years while he grew harder. Colder. He's buried his true self for so long that I no longer believe he remembers when he argued for helping the humans who have magic."

"Brandr is stoic like Con," Vaughn said. "In the time I've known your brother, I've found him fair and honest."

Cullen considered their words. He had spent barely five hours with either Brandr or Eurwen before he and other Dragon Kings were dispatched around the perimeter of the invisible shield dividing their land from the humans'. In that short time, he'd seen how strong the twins' bond was. He didn't want to be the one to sever that. "Then no one can know you helped, Eurwen."

"I kept things from Brandr before. I won't do it again," Eurwen said. "I promised I wouldn't do that again."

Vaughn kissed her forehead. "Sweetheart, if you tell your brother what you want to do, there could be a fight."

"It's worth it to save the bairns," Cullen interjected.

Eurwen nodded. "I agree. I'm going to call Brandr here."

"Uh…I doona think you need to," Vaughn said as he pointed over Cullen's shoulder.

Cullen turned around and saw the sunlight glinting off gold scales. At first, Cullen thought it was Con, since he was the King of Golds, but then Cullen caught the sight of the beige scales that ran the length of Brandr's underside. The three of them watched as Brandr soared above before dipping his wing to swing around and return to where they stood.

Brandr alighted close by, shifting to his human form instantly as he did. He looked at each of them before sighing loudly. "I'm going to regret this."

"What?" Cullen asked, confused.

Eurwen's face split into a wide smile. "I knew you wouldn't allow children to continue being harmed."

Cullen's head jerked to Brandr.

"Don't look so surprised," Brandr said with a wry grin. "Contrary to popular belief, I actually do have a heart."

Vaughn said, "As good as this is, we should bring Con in on this."

"He knows," Brandr replied. "I'm going to take up patrol here while Cullen is gone."

Cullen smiled as he looked at the other three. "I've been holding the ace up my sleeve. I'm glad I didna have to use it."

"What?" Eurwen asked.

"While I'm on the human side, I'll be able to search for our adversary," Cullen replied.

Brandr chuckled as he shook his head. "Con said you were the perfect King to send over. Now I know why."

Vaughn snorted. "And everyone thinks I've got the cunning mind."

"Oh, you do," Cullen said as they shared a smile.

Chapter Seven

Tamlyn walked the silent corridors of the ruins. She imagined that they had once been filled with people and voices. Now, they were silent as a tomb. She found the quiet soothing, allowing her thoughts to run free.

She, Sian, and Jenefer had told the kids they could run and play and be as loud as they wanted, but none did. Their trauma was too severe, especially for the older ones. It had taken her nearly all day to gain the name of the lad she'd last rescued. Peder wasn't sure of his new surroundings yet. The other children kept close to him for reassurance. They would give him more than any adult could.

Tamlyn ran her hand along the stones. Some looked as if they had been erected just a few days before, while others showed what the hands of time had done. She wished she had seen it when the sanctuary was at its best. Even now with some parts crumbled into ruins, she still saw the beauty that it had once been.

Something about the city allowed her to rest easy. She had once thought it was pure luck that had allowed her to stumble upon the hidden ruins. Yet the longer she was there, the more she began to wonder if she had been led here. Either way, she was glad she'd found it. And she would fight to remain.

Even if a Dragon King knew of it.

She inwardly grimaced when she thought about Cullen again. The damn dragon wouldn't stay out of her thoughts. How could someone she hadn't spent but a handful of minutes with, linger so vividly in her head? If she could get him out, she would.

Maybe.

No, she wouldn't.

"Ugh," she grumbled.

Why did Cullen have to be so fascinating? Handsome? Intriguing? Enticing?

When she was a little girl, after her escape from Stonemore, she used to look toward the divide between their lands and pray for a dragon to save her—even though she was supposed to fear them. She knew they had magic, and in her young mind, the perfect companion and savior was a dragon. None ever came, and she'd learned to survive on her own. Well, not entirely on her own. Jenefer and Sian had been by her side.

To discover that it wasn't just a dragon but a Dragon King that had come to her aid had been exciting and confusing. She wondered if she had made a mistake in sending him away. His offer had been unexpected. She, Sian, and Jenefer had survived so long together that they were leery of anyone else—especially someone from the other side.

Her close call with the soldiers, as well as the brineling, had her wondering how many more times she could get in and out of Stonemore before they caught her. When they *did* finally get their hands on her, her death wouldn't be quick. The priests would gleefully torture her. She had been in the hands of a priest before, and she never wanted to be back there.

A shudder went through her.

There was much she wanted to do with her life, but her trips to Stonemore would likely get her killed. She'd accepted her place because to deny it would only make things more difficult than they already were. Every life she saved brought a smile. She couldn't save them all, but she could save some, and that's exactly what she would do.

She meandered through the maze of passages until she came to one of the bigger rooms. It must have held a great many souls at one time. One of the faces from the entrance hall was directly across from her. It looked as if it emerged from the stones, the rock eyes open as if staring at her.

Tamlyn had spent many hours in this room, simply staring at the face. She sat in silence at times. Others, she talked. This room was a sanctuary for her. It was one of the first ones she had found, and she returned almost daily. The underground city was so large that every time she explored, she found something new.

Her confusion and worry had her longing for comfort. She lowered herself to the stone floor and crossed her legs, resting her hands upon her knees. She tried to clear her mind of all its thoughts to find some peace, but Cullen stubbornly remained.

"Damned dragon," she mumbled.

She shook her head. Every place she turned, every thought she had, returned to him. She began to consider that she had made a mistake in not accepting his help. It wasn't as if she could cross from her land into his and seek him out without retribution, and she wasn't that brave to face off against dragons. Even though, technically, part of their city was under the dragons' land. He had no reason to return after she had so callously sent him away.

Her pride had stopped her from accepting his help. That and the fear of having a Dragon King with her. They might both have magic, but she had learned from an early age to fear dragons. That kind of ingrained belief didn't go away easily.

She sighed and got to her feet to pace. The peace she usually found in the room eluded her. She rotated her shoulders, trying to dislodge the mounting anxiety settling between her shoulder blades. With each second, it increased until she had to do something to work off the energy or scream. Tamlyn began walking fast, but that wasn't enough. She started running through the halls and around corners.

She didn't stop until she found herself in the entrance hall. Tamlyn halted before the pool of water and leaned over with her hands on her knees as she caught her breath. She watched the never-ending water droplets fall into the pool from the roots above. The sound was calming.

Slowly, she straightened and lifted her gaze. Only to find herself staring at none other than Cullen. Fear mixed with excitement, warring to see which would come out on top. That knot between her shoulder blades was gone. Had it been the run? Or was it seeing the Dragon King again?

She wasn't sure she wanted to know the answer. No, she was *definitely* sure she didn't want the answer.

"Hi," he said from across the water.

One word, but that sexy voice sent shivers of awareness over her skin. It took Tamlyn a moment to find her own. "Hi."

"I know you told me no' to return, but I had to."

She licked her lips with a suddenly dry tongue. He stood so casually. As if he had been there for some time. "Oh?"

"I need your help," he said as he began slowly walking around the pool.

Tamlyn also moved toward him. The last thing she had expected to hear was that he needed her. "You want my help?"

"Doona sound so surprised, lass."

He couldn't call her lass again. It was…it did crazy things to her. Made her insides feel as if they were all mixed up, and sent her blood rushing hotly through her veins.

His lips tilted in a lopsided grin as the distance between them lessened. "I'm going to save some bairns. Want to help?"

She walked the last few steps to find herself within arm's length of him. Had he just said what she thought he did?

"Tamlyn?" he asked hesitantly as if she were addled.

She inwardly shook herself. "I heard you."

"Then say something."

"I'm not sure what to say."

He chuckled softly, and damn if she didn't find herself leaning toward him. Was he using some kind of magic? Why couldn't she seem to think straight? Why was she so ecstatic that he was there?

"Och, I didna think I'd ever find you speechless."

She blinked, completely absorbed by his voice. It didn't matter what he said. It all sounded so…deliciously sensual.

"Lass, you're beginning to worry me."

His words, and the frown lining his face, snapped her out of her head. She cleared her throat and took a step back, only to move forward again. It was like she had to be near him. "You want my help?"

"Aye. I thought we established that already. Did you hit your head this morning during the battle?"

She jerked her chin up, affronted. "No."

His brows drew together as he looked her over with his pale brown eyes. "You're acting peculiar."

Because of you, she barely admitted to herself. She certainly wouldn't tell him. "I'm surprised to see you. Not to mention your statement."

"Will you? Help me, that is?" he asked.

"You have no idea what you're getting into. I wasn't joking earlier. This could very well start a war."

He shook his head before she finished. "That willna happen. It can no' happen."

"I don't see how it won't."

"Leave that to me. I thought you wanted to save the kids."

"I do," she said tightly. "I have been."

Cullen bowed his blond head to her. "Then let me help."

This was the answer she needed. Tamlyn was sure of it. Still, she hesitated, unsure if this was the right thing to do. She hated those at Stonemore, especially the priests. They were cruel, brutal bastards who deserved a painful death. But who was she to decide that? She might get what she wanted and in turn bring about greater destruction than she wished.

"I'm going to do it one way or another," Cullen said. "I'd like to work with you since you can show me where to go and what to do. It'll be much better than me fumbling around."

"I don't think you've fumbled a day in your life," she said without thinking.

That brought another smile to his face, this one slow and daring.

Tamlyn hastily looked away. She didn't want to know what he was thinking. A laugh nearly burst from her lips at the outrageous lie. She desperately wanted to know what brought that sexy smile, but she was smart enough to keep her mouth closed.

Or maybe she was too much of a coward to get the answer.

"If I agree to this, we have to do things my way," she said.

He nodded. "I'm in your world. I'll follow your lead. I've promised my people that I willna start a war. I give you that same vow."

She really hoped he held to his word. But she had other worries. She had Jenefer to deal with. Sian had already made her thoughts about Cullen known. So had Jenefer, and the Amazon wouldn't be pleased that he was helping.

Tamlyn met his gaze. "How do I get in touch with you when I want to rescue a child?"

"I'll be right here."

Shock went through her. "Here? As in...*here?*"

"Aye." He didn't bother to hide his grin.

"I...uh...I'm not sure about that."

Cullen slowly looked around. "It seems this place is big enough. You'll never know I'm here."

She almost snorted. As if she could ever forget. She hadn't stopped thinking about him since that morning. And he'd left. How much worse would it be with him around?

"The sooner we get started, the better prepared we'll be," he said.

Tamlyn absently nodded, trying to come up with how to explain to Jenefer about their new guest.

"Do you hear the screams every night?"

She blinked and looked at him. "What? Uh...no. I don't know when they'll come."

"Is there any way we can find out who the children are before they're reported by the family? That way, we can get to them before they're handed over to the authorities."

"If there was, we would've done that years ago."

He crossed his arms over his chest. "How long have you been doing this?"

"Too long," she said softly.

"Your world and mine are verra different. It's separate for a good reason, but that doesna mean we are no' outraged at the thought of children sacrificed simply because they have magic."

She studied him for a long moment. "You know why our two worlds are separate?"

"I do."

No one had ever been able to give her an answer. The idea that she might uncover the big secret was too much to resist. "Will you tell me?"

He let out a long sigh. "Aye. First, tell me everything I need to do."

"Where do you want to start?"

"Stonemore. Lay out the city, tell me about the occupants, and describe anything I need to look for."

She chuckled. "You make it sound as if you'll go there during the day."

"Because I will."

"You can't," she said in astonishment.

He smiled. "Watch me."

Chapter Eight

He was in. But barely. Cullen knew he would have to tread carefully. Tamlyn was skittish and watchful. She would scrutinize every move he made. Then there were her other companions. Sian seemed amicable, but Jenefer didn't hide that she didn't want him anywhere near them.

"I suppose I should show you around," Tamlyn said.

He hid his smile. "Doona sound so excited."

She wrinkled her nose. "Sorry. It's just that we haven't had guests before."

Cullen dropped his arms to his sides. She was uncomfortable. Was it because he was near, or could it be because his presence might stir up conflict? It was probably both. He'd pushed her pretty hard since he arrived. It might be advisable to relent for a bit and let her grow accustomed to him. If they were to work together, they had to trust each other.

Tamlyn motioned for him to follow her. He fell into step with her as she took him to the opposite side of where he had seen her emerge. Dozens of questions rushed through his head, but he held back. For the moment. Instead, he took in the magnificence around him.

While the underground city was in decay, there was no denying its beauty or the fact that it had obviously been of great importance once. The grand architecture, incredible design, and carvings, along with the perfectly precise cuts on the stones left him eager to explore more of the ruins to see just how large the complex was.

The tall ceilings and wide corridors helped with being underground, giving the feel of lots of space. The sunlight pouring in through the tree roots from the main hall helped to spread light, but it wasn't enough—they had torches spaced throughout the hallways. Cullen had no problem seeing in the dark. Dragons could see just as well in the dark as they did in the light.

He paused next to a torch and inhaled. It wasn't a form of petrol like on Earth. In fact, he smelled nothing. He passed his fingers through the flames and watched them dance around his skin with barely any heat.

"It's not the kind of magic you're used to," Tamlyn said.

Cullen glanced at her to find she had paused and turned sideways to watch him. He lowered his arm to his side. "What do you mean?"

"We don't need to keep refilling the torches to keep them lit. Sian came up with a concoction that keeps the flames going as long as we need them to."

He took one more look at the torches before facing her. "Impressive. There's no heat, and it gives plenty of light. As for the ruins themselves, this place is astounding. How large is it?"

"We've been here for about two years, and I've not explored all of it yet in that time."

"Do you know what it used to be?" he asked as he came even with her.

Tamlyn fell into step with him as they continued. "Unfortunately, I don't. I left Stonemore when I was young and spent many years moving around and hiding. I've not spent a lot of time among others or in cities to gather such information."

"It's a shame it was abandoned. I'm curious about its history and why anyone would leave such a place."

"Maybe because it was on dragon land," she said and shot him a side-eye.

Cullen smiled. "Only some of it."

She turned left and then took another right before stopping in front of a door. "This room is one of the largest. You can use this one or any of the others along this corridor."

He walked through the doorway and moved his gaze over the dark, empty room. It was a good-sized chamber. "This will do nicely. Thanks."

"You'll be able to find your way here?"

"Aye. I promise to stay out of your way, though I do have a request."

She gave him a flat look as if she wasn't surprised. "What would that be?"

"If you hear the screams again, shout my name. I'll hear you and catch up, but you shouldna go to the city alone."

"You sound like Jenefer."

"You're capable, but your friend is concerned for your safety. After what I saw this morning, I agree with her. I'm here to help. So is she. Use us."

Tamlyn's lips twisted. "I'm not sure Jenefer will want to work with you."

"I'll bring her around."

"She won't make it easy for you."

He grinned and walked to her. "Jenefer is a warrior. She has taken it upon herself to guard no' just you and Sian, but this place and the bairns. Anyone new who comes in could cause more harm than good."

Tamlyn's brows snapped together. "How do you know that?"

"*I'm* a warrior. We see it in others like us. Jenefer carries a heavy burden, but she has done her job well. You three have no' only survived but thrived."

"We all pitched in."

He drew in a breath. "Will you show me more of the ruins? I'd also like to learn about Stonemore."

"That city should be destroyed," she said tightly.

"Is it the city or those ruling it?"

She shrugged and moved into the hallway. "Those ruling, I suppose. But taking out one or two people isn't going to change anything. The rituals and customs have been a part of them for too long. Nothing will stop them now."

"Oh, I doona know about that," Cullen said as he thought about other such people who had been dealt with on Earth.

Tamlyn didn't turn back the way they had come. Instead, she continued onward. "Stonemore is in tiers and built along a mountain. It's protected by a half-moon-shaped range of mountains—the Tunris—on either side, and a forest—Ferdon Woods—before it."

"How far is it from the forest to the bottom of the city?"

She thought about that for a moment then came to a halt. After eyeing the length of the hallway, she said, "From here to the final torch."

Cullen imagined that to be about a quarter of a mile. Not a great distance, but not close, either. "I gather the city is gated?"

"Oh, yes. The wall surrounding the city is very thick," she said and started walking again.

He glanced inside other rooms as they passed, discovering they were as empty as the one she had shown him. "How many levels?"

"Eight. They hold the children in the temple on the far-left side of the fourth level. It's where the priests prepare themselves for the executions."

Cullen curled his lip in agitation. "Priests? What kind of priests?"

"The kind you want to stay away from."

"They murder children. How scary can they be?"

Tamlyn halted and turned to him. "Do you have priests?"

"The humans on my realm follow many religions. Too many to go through and explain. We do have priests, but they can go by many names depending on the culture and denomination."

"Do your priests go into battle?"

Cullen quirked a brow thinking of the Templars. "Battle? There was once such a sect, but no' anymore."

"Ours do. They are soldiers before they are chosen by the Divine, the ruler of Stonemore, to be a priest. They give up any family they have and devote the rest of their lives to the defense and order of Stonemore. Once chosen, they either accept their new position, or they're killed."

"They doona have a choice in the matter?"

Tamlyn shook her head, her curls moving with her.

"And how does the Divine choose?"

"No one knows. He's had an iron rule over Stonemore for decades."

Cullen would like to have a few words with the priests and ruler, but if he were to keep his promise of not starting a war, he would have to steer clear of them. That might prove harder than expected, especially the more he learned about Stonemore.

Tamlyn glanced at him. "I have a favor."

"What is it?"

"I'd like to tell Jenefer and Sian about you being here and why before they see you."

He chuckled. "In other words, you want me to stay out of the way."

"To be blunt, yes."

"Consider it done. Should I remain on this side?"

"That would be perfect."

After she gave him specifics about the places to stay away from, Cullen watched her walk away. His gaze lingered on the sway of her hips. She had an allure that he found both tempting and terrifying. Others at Dreagan had yearned to find mates. Not him. He had been content just as he was. Not that he didn't have an entanglement every now and again. A man had needs, after all. But more than that? Never. He didn't allow himself to ever get close enough to a female.

He pivoted and turned his gaze—and his mind—from Tamlyn. While he walked through the corridors, he inspected every room. Some were small, some large, and some in between. Some had stone benches along the outer edges, but most were as barren as the one Tamlyn had shown him.

As he came to a junction in the hallway, he decided to go left. It would keep him further from Tamlyn and the others. His thoughts moved from the unknown evil attacking the dragons and the reason he and the other Dragon Kings were on Zora, to the plight of the children with magic, to the ruins he found himself in. The more he learned about Zora, the more he fell in love with the realm.

Light caught his attention. He halted and turned his head to the left. His lips parted in awe as he walked through a tall archway and into a vast courtyard with smooth walls. In the middle stood four towers about fifteen feet high with a center tower that soared over them.

Cullen craned his head back to follow the center tower. Light from above shone down on the courtyard, the luminescent stones beneath his feet bouncing the light back up. Curious, Cullen walked to the center tower. The flawless cut of the stones, the way they had been meticulously laid with such skill and reverence, was difficult to miss or deny.

The carvings on the outside of the towers were stunning—human figures framed with decorative archways, phases of the moon, and various animals. Inside the tower was nothing but a staircase. Cullen followed it up to the top to seek out the source of the light. When he reached the summit, he was shocked to discover the same stones cut into smaller octagonal shapes, surrounding a single three-foot crystal pillar. The crystal reflected off the stones, flooding everything with light. It was ingenious.

Cullen returned to the courtyard, but he wasn't ready to leave. He walked around until he spotted a couple of circles cut out of the stone walls, big enough for him to stand in. He sat in the depression of one sphere and laced his fingers behind his head while stretching his legs out to rest on the upward curve. He barely paid attention to the hallway the opening showed him. Instead, he kept his focus on the towers and light. The longer he was there, the more he could imagine he was outside, the light was so bright.

He had no idea how long he lay there, lost in thought before he heard footsteps approaching. Then Tamlyn stood before him.

"There you are. I've been searching for you."

He eyed her. "Do you know what makes the light at the top?"

"A crystal. It's been here since we arrived."

"Aye," he replied with a smile. "Did you talk to your friends?"

She couldn't hold his gaze. "Sian was with the kids, and I couldn't find Jenefer."

"I told you I wouldna leave this area."

"I know. It's just...well, I want to know why we're separate from the dragons."

Cullen had promised her. It didn't matter how long ago it was or that the dragons had been found safe. It still hurt to speak about it. He lowered his arms, swung his legs to the side, and pushed himself to his feet.

"It isna a good tale."

She held his gaze. "I'd really like to know if you would share."

He motioned for her to take his seat. If he were going to pull up those memories, he had to move around. "Our realm is called Earth. For countless years, the dragons ruled. There was only us and other animals. We covered the entire globe, every continent, in every climate. Our numbers were vast, and the land plentiful. Magic wasna just part of us, but also the planet. We found the source of the magic and made that area our home. It's where the Dragon Kings gathered. We call it Dreagan. To feel the force of the magic is breathtaking."

"You can feel it?"

Cullen turned his head to her and smiled. "It's so thick in the Dragonwood, you can almost scoop it up with your hand."

"That sounds amazing."

"The magic chooses the Dragon Kings. It looks deep into the hearts of all dragons and finds the ones with the most magic, the most power, and the purest hearts to lead their clans. The magic chose dragons to protect Earth and the beings that lived on it. Things were no' perfect, but they were good. But everything changed one day with the arrival of humans."

Her dark brows drew together. "You mean they just showed up? Like the infants do here?"

"Aye. Except they were adults. They had no memory of who they were, and no magic. The Kings gathered before them. Before we knew it, we began to shift to their form. We were able to understand their language, and by shifting, we could speak with them. Constantine, the

King of Dragon Kings, gave them protection since they were defenseless. We helped them build shelters and showed them how to hunt for food. We accepted them into our realm, and they accepted us. Some Kings even took the females as lovers. But that peace didna last. The mortals bred at a rapid rate and kept encroaching on our land. Dragons ate them at times, and they hunted and killed dragons. We gave more land to them, but it was only a matter of time before they wanted even more."

Tamlyn pressed her lips together. "That doesn't sound fair."

"I'm sure it depends on who you ask," he said with a rueful twist of his lips. "Things went on like that for a while. We were making it work. Then, one of the Kings fell in love with a human woman. Ulrik wanted to marry her. His uncle was bitter over no' being a King himself, so he turned the female against Ulrik, urging her to kill Ulrik on their wedding night."

Tamlyn's hazel eyes bulged. "Please tell me she didn't."

"Con overheard one of their conversations. Ulrik was his best friend, and Con wouldna stand to have him betrayed in such a fashion. Con gathered the rest of us and informed us what was going on. So, we hunted her down and killed her."

"That's extreme," Tamlyn said in a soft voice. "She hadn't done anything yet."

Cullen shrugged. "It seemed the right thing to do at the time. None of us realized it would change the course of everything. Tensions were already high between humans and dragons by that point. And Ulrik was furious over what'd happened. Angry at us, angry at the humans. He took his Silvers and began attacking the mortals. At first, only a few Kings joined him. It wasna long before most did. We wanted our realm back the way it was. Unfortunately, that started the war Con had been struggling to prevent. It took some time, but Con managed to get us back to his side, one by one. Some Kings sent their dragons to protect the humans at all costs, but that was the worst thing they could've done. The mortals attacked those dragons, and because the Kings ordered them to protect the humans, the dragons didna defend themselves. So many dragons were murdered that day."

Cullen had to pause because the emotions were so heavy. Recalling those memories put him right back in them as if he were reliving it a second time. He squeezed his eyes closed, but he could still hear the dragons' scared roars, the screams of the dying humans, and the Kings' frantic calls.

His eyes snapped open when he felt a hand on his arm. Cullen looked over to find Tamlyn beside him. Her touch eased the vise around his chest. No one had ever comforted him in such a way. He found that he liked her touch. He wanted more of it.

Sadness filled her face. Her voice was soft as she asked, "What happened?"

"Whatever truce we'd had with the mortals was gone. The Kings recognized that we had two choices. We could wipe the world of the humans so we could live in peace, or we could send the dragons away."

She shook her head, no words leaving her lips.

"The magic chose each King because of our purity. If we killed innocents, we would no longer be us. We had vowed to protect our realm and those who lived on it. Murdering the mortals would turn us into something we didna want to think about."

Tamlyn dropped her hand slowly from his arm. "You thought the answer was sending your kind away?"

"We wanted to give them a chance for peace and happiness while we sorted things out on Earth. We always intended to bring them back."

"Did you?"

Cullen shook his head. "Once the last dragon was gone, we put up a barrier around Dreagan so the mortals would stay away, and we hid away for centuries, waiting until our memory became myth and legend. When we came out, we realized that our hope of bringing our dragons back was gone. The humans had taken over the realm. We had to hide who we were. Even though we had magic and could wipe them out with barely a thought, we hid. Even now, we only fly at night so we aren't seen, and we keep our magic to ourselves."

"The dragons here are yours?"

"Their descendants, aye," he said with a nod. "We only recently discovered this realm."

She made a sound of confusion. "Then how did the dragons find this place?"

"They had help from a goddess, who created this realm specifically for them. She made it look as much like Earth as she could. Like my realm, there were only dragons here for a time."

"Then humans began showing up," she added.

Cullen sighed, nodding. "Brandr and Eurwen, those who rule the dragons here, are the twins of Constantine and his mate, Rhi—a royal Light Fae. They knew what'd happened on Earth, and they wanted to ensure that it didna repeat on Zora."

Tamlyn nodded in understanding. "Which is why there is a barricade and the fear of dragons."

"It's why the twins wanted to keep the dragons safe and the humans to their own plots of land. They also enforced that there wouldna be any more land. If your kind outgrew what they had, it was their problem."

"I can see why after your story. Making us fear the dragons ensured we didn't cross the barrier."

Cullen paused. "Brandr or Eurwen spoke to the humans to have them fear crossing onto dragon land, but not the dragons themselves."

"Where did that come from if not from them?"

"Good question."

Chapter Nine

To say Tamlyn was shocked by Cullen's story was an understatement. She had imagined all sorts of reasons for why the humans and dragons didn't mingle, but she'd never expected to hear anything so tragic. So many things made sense now.

What confused her was the terror among her kind for the dragons. If they had always been kept isolated, where did the fear originate from? Because it had to start from somewhere. It wasn't just those in Stonemore who were scared of dragons. It was all humans on Zora. Her kind either feared them or hated them.

Or both.

"I'm saddened and appalled by your story," she told him.

He shot her a dejected smile. "As am I. Our honor kept us from protecting our way of life and the dragons."

"You've returned to the dragons now."

"No' as you think. We're only visiting."

Her face went slack. "I don't understand. You said you must hide on Earth. Why wouldn't you live here now that you've found your dragons once more?"

"Every color dragon was a clan. Each clan had a King. When we sent the dragons from Earth, they no longer had Kings to lead them. They had to sort things out for themselves until the twins found them. They've lived for many thousands of years without clans."

She wrinkled her nose. "You said Brandr and Eurwen rule here."

"That's right."

"And they're Con and Rhi's twins."

Cullen grinned. "You're wondering how they've been here, but we were no'."

"I am," she said with a nod.

"It's a verra long, convoluted story, but the condensed version is that the twins were taken from Rhi's womb early in her pregnancy after she was injured."

Tamlyn eyed him. "That isn't possible."

"It is if a goddess does it. Death, the same goddess who created this realm, made the decision to save Rhi and the twins. However, the twins refused to return to Rhi's womb. Death had no choice but to keep the children safe until they were born. I believe they knew their destiny was on Zora, and that would never have happened if they had been born on Earth."

Tamlyn rubbed her forehead. "Shite. That's a lot to take in."

"For countless centuries, Eurwen and Brandr made sure we couldna find the dragons. When Death finally told Con and Rhi about the twins, they desperately tried to see their children. It was Eurwen who eventually allowed it. She is now mated to a Dragon King, Vaughn."

Tamlyn bit her lip, confused with all the storylines and names. "So, Con is King of Dragon Kings, and Rhi is a Light Fae. That means Brandr and Eurwen aren't full-blooded dragons."

Cullen nodded in agreement. "They're half-dragon and half-Fae."

"You live alongside the Fae?"

"Somewhat. There are Light and Dark Fae. They came to Earth after a civil war destroyed their realm. All Fae are beautiful creatures and irresistible to humans. The Dark sustain themselves by feeding on mortals' souls while having sex. The only decent thing about that is that the humans experience untold ecstasy and doona know they're dying. The Light restrain themselves and engage in only one sexual experience with a human, though that one time makes it impossible for the mortals to find fulfillment with humans again."

"How do you know the difference between Light and Dark Fae?"

"The Light have silver eyes and black hair. The Dark have red eyes and silver in their black hair. The more evil they do, the more silver they have."

Tamlyn shivered at the image his words invoked. "Does that mean Brandr and Eurwen aren't a Dragon King or Dragon Queen? You haven't mentioned Queens."

"Brandr is a King, and Eurwen is a Queen. They can shift from dragon to human. That's what sets them apart. Male dragons are bigger than females. It makes them physically stronger, which is what prevented the magic on Earth from choosing a female to lead a clan."

"I suppose that makes sense," she agreed. Tamlyn turned and walked to the wall seat she had found Cullen lying on and sat. "I'd like to say that things could be different here on Zora, but with so many of my kind hating anything to do with magic, I can't see that happening since dragons *are* magic."

Cullen shook his head sadly. "It willna. Dragon Kings and Queens are used to dealing with humans, with many of my brethren taking them as mates. But the dragons here despise humans too much."

"We've not given them a reason to trust us. The same could be said for them. But we aren't the same ones who caused the problems on your realm. Neither are the dragons the same ones who left Earth."

His pale brown eyes held hers. "You may no' have been run out of your home, but the priests were going to take your life. How do you feel about them?"

"You know how I feel," she bit out.

"If you have children or grandchildren, would you pass on your story?"

She drew in a sharp breath. "Absolutely. I'd want them to know what kind of evil there is."

"What of the priests? The ones who harmed you would be long dead. Would you have your descendants carry your hatred?"

"My plight is different."

Cullen shook his head. "It isna. To the dragons, humans are selfish, greedy beings who care for nothing but themselves."

"Not all of us."

"If there were no barrier between dragon land and mortals, would your kind spread over the realm?"

Tamlyn lowered her gaze as her shoulders slumped. "Without a doubt."

"If the dragons so wanted, they could fly over every human city and annihilate them all. There would be nothing left but ash. Yet, they doona."

She slid her gaze to him. "Because they're ordered not to?"

"Partly. They want to be left alone, but it hasna happened."

"It has," she said, affronted that he would claim otherwise.

He briefly lowered his eyes to the ground. "Do you know Orgate?"

"I've heard of the city."

"There were those there who had been capturing dragons and

torturing them for years, using the dragons' magic to strengthen theirs, and preventing others from using magic within the city."

Tamlyn was glad she was sitting, the shock was so great. "I–I don't understand. Those without don't want magic in their cities."

"Unless the leader of a city happens to *have* magic and manages to keep it from everyone."

"It's so preposterous that I can barely believe it."

"Well, I don't believe," Jenefer said as she strode into the courtyard.

Tamlyn jumped to her feet in surprise. She glanced at Cullen, but he didn't seem surprised to see Jenefer. Sian stood a few steps behind the warrior and smiled in greeting at Cullen. He bowed his head to both women.

"What is he doing here?" Jenefer demanded.

Tamlyn licked her lips. This isn't at all how she'd wanted to tell her friends. Her lips parted, but before she could utter a syllable, Sian spoke.

"One of the children said they heard a male voice. We decided to check it out," she said.

Tamlyn sighed and met Jenefer's glare. "He returned earlier, offering aid again."

"And you accepted, knowing how I felt?" Jenefer demanded.

Tamlyn thought about all the reasons to argue for Cullen, but she decided against it. "I did. We could use the help."

"Speak for yourself," Jenefer snapped.

Sian put a hand on Jenefer's arm and glanced at her before saying to Tamlyn, "We just wish you would've spoken with us first before deciding."

"You two make decisions all the time without talking to me. Why is this any different?" Tamlyn asked. "Whether we like it or not, having Cullen aid us will be good."

Jenefer rolled her eyes. "You don't know him. This could all be a setup."

"Maybe, but it's a chance I'm willing to take." Tamlyn blew out a long breath. "We've managed to save a few, but not as many as we could. Think how many more children we could free."

Sian clasped her hands in front of her. "I'm not against Cullen helping—"

"Thank you," Tamlyn said.

"But," Sian said, her gaze hard, "how? It isn't as if you can walk into the city and start taking children."

Jenefer crossed her arms over her chest and turned her attention to Cullen. "Why are you doing this?"

"As I told you earlier, the bairns. They can no' help being born with magic or abilities. They shouldna be condemned to death because there are those who doona wish to accept that." Cullen faced Jenefer. "I've given my word to my friends that I willna instigate a war. I gave that same vow to Tamlyn, and I give it to both of you."

Jenefer shrugged her shoulders slightly. "Pretty words. I'd like to believe them, but I think there's more."

"There is."

Tamlyn snapped her head to Cullen, furious that he hadn't told her. "What?"

He swung his gaze to her. "It isna a secret. I was about to tell you when your friends appeared."

"Tell us now," Jenefer ordered.

Tamlyn saw a muscle twitch in Cullen's jaw, but he remained calm. She had to give him credit because Jenefer was pushing him.

"Recently, there have been attacks on dragons coming from your side of the barrier," he said.

Sian shook her head. "Who would be that stupid? I take it they've been caught."

"What's a few spears thrown?" Jenefer asked with a roll of her eyes.

"Several dragons were killed," Cullen replied, anger tinting his voice. "Both Brandr and Eurwen were also attacked, but they managed to survive."

Jenefer dropped her arms, her expression easing from its hard lines. "We heard nothing about that. Do you know who it was?"

Cullen shook his head. "No one was seen."

"How is that possible?" Tamlyn asked.

Cullen looked at her. "That's what I aim to find out."

"In other words, you're really here to find those who harmed your kind," Jenefer stated.

Cullen closed his eyes for a moment. "I'm here for both. There's no reason I can no' take care of both issues while I'm here."

"And if you're found out?" Sian asked.

He lifted one shoulder in a shrug. "That willna happen. But if it does, I'll make sure I have no association with any of you if that's what you're worried about."

"I'm not," Tamlyn said. She looked at her friends when they gawked at her. "Think about it. Do you know what having a Dragon King on our side could do for us?"

"You trust him?" Jenefer demanded. "After everything we've been raised to believe about dragons and Dragon Kings?"

Tamlyn hesitated, glancing at Cullen. His pale brown eyes met hers. A tremor went through her. The fear was still there, but she couldn't deny that something pulled her to him. She had learned so much already. "Yes."

"He saved Tamlyn and Pedar this morning," Sian said.

Tamlyn could see Sian agreed with her. She held Jenefer's gaze. "You can't deny I'm right. His arrival might be exactly what is needed to band everyone who has magic together. There's no reason we can't have our own cities and live in peace."

"I thought there was a city like that already," Cullen said.

Jenefer irritably said, "Highvale, but not everyone makes it there."

"Those with and without magic should be able to live together," Sian said.

Tamlyn snorted. "That's wishful thinking. At the very least, when children are discovered to have magic, someone at Highvale should be notified so the child can be brought there and not subjected to slavery, banishment, or death."

"What you're suggesting would bring on war," Jenefer said. "The instant the others think we might rise against them, they'll come after us."

Cullen snorted as he crossed his arms over his chest. "Let them, if they're that stupid. They come with weapons, but you all have magic."

"Not everyone with magic can defend themselves," Sian replied. "I have knowledge of science and how to use chemicals and metals to create things, but many consider that magic. While Jenefer has trained us so we have some fighting skills, neither of us has magic for defense."

Not for the first time, Tamlyn wished she had some kind of magic. Something that would be more useful in keeping her and others safe from harm. She looked at Cullen to find his eyes on her. His face didn't give away his thoughts, much as she wished otherwise. Was he wondering if he'd made a mistake? She hoped not. Because she was really glad that he was here.

That certainly wasn't something she'd ever thought to think about a Dragon King. It was odd, but the fear that had nearly choked her when she first discovered who he was had begun to diminish.

Chapter Ten

Cullen was so used to having magic, he forgot that not everyone could wield it as they pleased. Once it had been pointed out to him, he was more amazed than ever that the trio had managed to elude capture and remain alive, all while rescuing the children.

"These ruins should be shielded from others finding it. I can do that," he offered. "It will ensure that those inside remain safe."

"That would be amazing," Sian said excitedly.

At the same time, Jenefer said, "We don't need that."

Tamlyn sighed and shot Jenefer a hard look. "Don't be stupid. This isn't just about us. It's about the children."

"Think about it," Sian said as she turned to look up at Jenefer. "No soldiers or those without magic will be able to find us. We can stay here for as long as we want. You're always worried about someone getting in one of the other entrances and finding us. This will take that burden off you."

The fury tightening Jenefer's face told Cullen that he was making matters worse, not better. That's when he realized he was stepping on her toes. She was the one who had protected the other two. His solution took her out of the equation. He had no intention of returning to the other side of the barrier without completing his missions. Which meant he had to fix this.

"You've done a fine job protecting this place, Jenefer," Cullen said. "Let me help so you can put your focus on other things."

Tamlyn smiled at Jenefer. "You'd finally be able to sleep the entire night instead of patrolling all the time."

"You can spend more time training Tamlyn and me," Sian added.

Tamlyn then said, "And hunt. I know how you love to hunt for food."

Sian looked from Tamlyn to Jenefer and nodded. "This place is huge. With the shield in place, we could spend more time together."

"Fine," Jenefer bit out, but she didn't seem as angry as before.

Cullen would have to tread carefully around the warrior. "I doona want to cause contention."

"Too late," Jenefer replied sharply.

"Use me and my magic," he continued, ignoring her words. "What you three have done has worked, but from what I witnessed this morning, that could end quickly. It's the bairns that matter."

Something he said worked because Jenefer's expression softened. She looked at Sian and took her hand. Sian smiled brightly and rose on tiptoe as the two shared a kiss.

When Cullen looked at Tamlyn, she mouthed, *"Thank you."* He smiled in reply. This was a small victory, but he knew that Jenefer wouldn't make it easy. There would be other obstacles, and he would get over them when they cropped up.

Jenefer caught his eye. "Can you shield this place now?"

Cullen nodded as he called up his magic. With a thought, he put a protective defense around the entire compound. "It's done."

"Oh," Sian replied, disappointment on her face. "I thought we'd get to actually see the magic."

Jenefer quirked a blond brow. "How do we know you actually did it?"

"The shield is invisible, much like the one dividing the humans' land from the dragons'. We will be able to see the entrances, but no one else will," he explained.

Tamlyn's lips curved into a soft smile. "Thank you."

"Will this shield actually keep people out, or can they walk through it like we can walk through to the dragon's side?" Jenefer asked.

"Jenefer," Tamlyn admonished.

Cullen held up his hand to Tamlyn. "She has a right to her questions, and it's a legitimate one. It's the same type of barrier we use around our home on Earth. Others will be compelled to stay away, but if they want to get through badly enough, they will. If that happens, I've made it so we'll all be alerted to that fact."

"Thank you," Jenefer said after a brief pause. Then she turned on her heel and walked away.

Sian beamed at him. "She won't admit it, but you've taken a great weight off her shoulders. Thanks."

He returned her smile before she followed Jenefer out of the courtyard. Leaving him alone with Tamlyn once more. Cullen liked her company. Her tenacity and bravery astounded him. To have put her life on the line again and again without the use of magic to defend herself shocked him to his very core.

"What?" she asked with a frown. "You're staring."

"I made the mistake of assuming you had magic to defend yourself. When Sian pointed out that neither of you were able to do that, it made me think how you've put yourself in danger by going after the children."

Tamlyn shrugged. "I have to. If I don't, they'll die."

"Even so, you've lost some, have you no'?"

"Yes," she said softly.

He walked to the opening in the wall and sat before motioning for her to join him. "These priests must know someone is taking the children."

"They do, but they don't know who."

"How do you get into the temple?"

Her lips twisted as she sat beside him. "I climb the temple wall after I sneak into the city."

"You do what?" he asked in disbelief.

"I can't exactly walk inside the temple. The priests are everywhere. I'd never get past them to get upstairs to where the kids are kept at the top."

Cullen rubbed his forehead in agitation. "Tell me the wall isn't verra high."

"I can, but it'd be a lie."

"Bloody hell," he murmured and jumped to his feet to pace. He halted and faced her. "How do you get the kids out?"

She couldn't meet his gaze when she said, "They climb onto my back."

"For fuck's sake. I'm beginning to think you are no' brave. You have a death wish."

"You think I'm brave?"

Something in her voice made him pause. He looked to find a delighted expression on her face. No one had ever looked at him with such pleasure before. For all the things he griped about, he'd had a good existence. Tamlyn and others like her ran for their lives, stopping along the way to help those they could. She sacrificed everything to help those who couldn't help themselves. Brave? She was that and more. She was fucking incredible.

"Aye, lass. You are. I doona know many who would do the same in your shoes."

She lowered her chin to her chest, but not before he saw her smile widen in delight. "I do what I have to do."

"You go above and beyond. I'm hoping that with my help, we can make things easier and safer for all involved."

Tamlyn lifted her head and nodded. "I'm glad you came back."

"Me, too."

She licked her lips and asked, "Is there anything else you want to know?"

"What is Jenefer's magic? I take it she has some."

"Not in the way you or I have it. Jenefer's magic is in her sword. All Amazons have magical weapons."

Cullen should've known that Jenefer was an Amazon. Her height, her warrior nature, the way she dressed and carried herself had declared who she was. "Are there many Amazons on Zora?"

"You must understand that things are different for us. We know only what the family who takes us in knows. Then, if you have magic, you're cast aside. You're made to feel as if you are unworthy of love or acceptance, that you're…tainted, somehow. When the magic begins to manifest, you're terrified because you have no idea what it means. I didn't know what was happening to me, so I told the couple acting as my parents. They shared a look, immediately took me to the temple, and shoved me into the hands of the priests."

Cullen couldn't begin to imagine what sort of hell Tamlyn had withstood. No one, but most especially a child, should ever have to go through something so ghastly or malicious. "What did they do?"

"Studied me for days," she said with a mocking twist of her lips. "They put me through various tests. They asked me over and over again what kind of magic I had. If they knew, they never told me. I wouldn't know now if it wasn't for the Banshee who rescued me."

In the silence that followed, Cullen returned to his seat and looked at Tamlyn. "Was it the same for your friends?"

"Sian has a twin. They happened to live near a city that paid handsomely for anyone who had Alchemist children. The family they were with, sold them to a man who forced them to make potions to keep him and his wife young and beautiful. Sian and Mair tried to escape once. Guards chased and cornered them. Mair gave herself up so Sian could get free. We've been trying to find a way to rescue her ever since."

Cullen looked at the stones on the ground beneath his feet. "How long ago did Sian escape?"

"Five years. The city isn't the problem. It's the house where her sister is kept."

Cullen slowly released a breath. "And Jenefer?"

Tamlyn turned sideways and sat cross-legged, facing him. "The family that took her in knew she was different when she kept growing. Everyone treated her badly for it. One day, a group of older boys attacked her in her village. No one stepped in to help. She was able to defeat all five of them, but they ran her out of town because of it. She was only ten at the time. The way she explained it was that she felt this *pull*, and she followed it. It led her to a small group of women like her. They told her what she was."

"And her weapon? How did she get that?"

"She won't talk about it. Not to me, at least. She might have told Sian. What I do know is she found it while with the Amazons."

Cullen ran his hand over his lower face. "Infants arriving from some unknown place. Humans with and without magic. Magical weapons. What did Erith do when she created this realm?"

"Erith?"

"Death's real name."

"Do you think she could answer your questions?"

He shrugged. "I'd love to find out."

"You can contact her?"

Cullen smiled at her surprise. "Aye, but that doesna mean she'll appear. I want to find out more before I call for her."

"You really think we can do this?"

"If you mean rescue the bairns? Definitely."

She raised her brows. "And the other? The foe you seek?"

"Whoever or whatever that is, it can kill dragons. That may be all it wants, but it could be after something else."

"You're helping us. We'll help you."

He stared into her hazel eyes. The urge to lean in and kiss her was great. He didn't dare do it because one taste wouldn't be enough. He would want more.

That wasn't true. He would want it *all*.

Cullen had never met anyone with such strength *and* vulnerability as Tamlyn. The need to protect her was as undeniable as his attraction. He couldn't recall the last time he had felt such a strong tie to anyone. Usually, he would find an excuse and leave when he got too close. He hadn't been with her a full day, and yet it seemed as if he had known her for years. That should scare him. Yet, it didn't. It felt...right.

"You're staring again," she whispered.

"So are you," he pointed out.

Her lips softened into a smile that was altogether too sexy.

His blood heated as he imagined how soft her mouth would be against his, how pliant her body would feel against his. Kiss her? Hell, he wanted to devour her.

He was so fucked.

Chapter Eleven

Tamlyn couldn't make sense of the sensations whirling through her. So many years of fearing dragons didn't just vanish. But then there was this attraction, the need to be close to Cullen. She wanted to put her hand on him again. One touch against his muscular arm simply wasn't enough.

She wanted to run her hands over every inch of him. To strip away his odd clothes and feast her eyes on the hard body beneath. His shirt molded to him, giving her an idea of what she sought. And that tease only made her palms itch to reach for him.

Her breath caught when she saw his gaze lower to her mouth. When she parted her lips, he swallowed before lifting his brown eyes filled with desire. Tamlyn was out of her depth. Her brain told her to run away, to put distance between them so she could think clearly again.

But her body wanted something altogether different. It needed to know his touch, longed to know what it felt like to be in his arms.

Hungered for him.

She couldn't catch her breath. Warmth flooded her. She lost herself in the beautiful pale brown pools of his eyes. Why did he make her feel safe? Was it magic? Was he using some kind of spell to make her want him? At the moment, she didn't care. She was too caught up in the wonderful, blissful feelings.

The distance between them lessened. She didn't know if she had moved or if it was Cullen—and she didn't care. The yearning within her was too powerful to ignore.

His large palm slid against her cheek. Her heart leapt when his fingers sank into her hair. As his face grew near, she closed her eyes. Then his mouth brushed hers. It was so gentle at first that she wasn't sure if it was real. Then he was back, his lips supple yet demanding. His other hand came around the back of her neck to gently hold her. The feel of him, the taste of him, was as if she had been waiting her whole life for the kiss.

She moaned softly when his tongue slid against hers. Tamlyn parted her lips and gripped his shoulders as their tongues found each other, twisting, turning, gliding. Heat pulsed through her. He deepened the kiss, sweeping her into a frenzy of desire and pleasure that she never wanted to end.

To her disappointment, he ended the kiss. They were both breathing hard when he leaned back to look at her. She had to blink several times to bring him into focus. How could one kiss send her spiraling into such carnal need?

Tamlyn jumped to her feet and moved a safe distance away from Cullen before she ripped off his clothes—though she wasn't sure the other side of Zora would be far enough away. She squeezed her eyes closed and blinked them open. He watched her, making no attempt to hide his desire. Her heart leapt at the sight of it.

No one had ever looked at her in such a way before. It did something to her that she couldn't name. And all she wanted to do was return to her seat, lean in, and kiss him again. What would be the harm?

Cullen stood. She searched his face, trying to see if she could determine what he was thinking. Unfortunately, she couldn't decipher anything. If she was going to be around him, Tamlyn had to learn to read Cullen. If she continued as she was, she'd likely make some kind of huge error.

Like kissing him again. She knew in the depths of her very soul that she was meant to share her body with him. She'd never known anything with such certainty before, and it frightened her.

"You still fear me?" he asked.

Not in the way he thought, but maybe it was better if he believed she did. For both of them. "Yes."

"I'll win you over eventually," he said with a grin.

She took another step back after seeing his smile. How could he get more gorgeous?

He ran a hand over his beard. "This might be a good time for you to describe how others are dressed in Stonemore."

Clothes. That was a safe thing to talk about. "Yes."

He frowned at her and waited.

Tamlyn shook herself. She had to stop acting insane. After a deep breath that she slowly released, she thought about the city. "There is abject poverty living close to extreme wealth."

"Sadly, that isna condensed to Stonemore or even this realm."

She didn't like hearing that. Were all humans the same? Surely, not. "The wealthy prefer fitted dark blue garments. The lower classes wear greens, browns, reds, and oranges. The tops will typically be long-sleeved with plunging necklines. Most everyone wears breeches, but some women choose long skirts. Shoes range from sandals to boots. Like mine," she added when she glanced at his.

Cullen grinned. "Mine would be a giveaway."

"I almost wish they could see you dressed like this. I'd love to see their reaction."

He crossed his arms over his chest, a small frown marring his forehead. "Your people travel, correct? It wouldna be out of the ordinary for someone from another city to visit Stonemore."

"There are visitors, yes. The city has good trade, but they're not very welcoming to outsiders or newcomers."

"Because they have something to hide?"

"Because they're narrow-minded arseholes who can't see that our world is bigger than they are."

Cullen shot her a wide smile. "Nicely put."

She couldn't hold back her answering smile. "Why do you want to know about travelers?"

"In case there's a need to think fast while we're there."

"I wish I never had to return," she said as anger rose to choke her. "It's a vile city."

He dropped his arms and slowly walked around the courtyard but remained near her. "You could...remove...those in charge, but it wouldna change the city."

"I know. The tiny minds have had control for too long and brainwashed everyone. I'm sure some without magic believe as we do, but they dare not speak out for fear of reprisal. I blame it on the religion. The Priests of Innus are utterly devoted to their deity, who speaks through one person—the Divine."

Cullen snorted. "He's no' full of himself, is he?"

"No one's ever seen him. He doesn't come out of his palace at the top of the city. No one but the priests and guards are allowed inside the palace."

"Surely, he has guests. A wife? Children?"

"If he does, I've never heard of it. People whisper his name. Whatever he says is taken as fact. Those who live in Stonemore believe he has a connection to a deity."

Cullen's gaze narrowed slightly. "Tell me of this god."

She almost gagged thinking about how the religion had been forced down her throat as a child. "There are three main gods and many lesser ones, but they're ruled by one. Innus. The followers believe that he created this realm and brings each of us here as infants to fulfill a destiny."

"A destiny about what?"

She shrugged. "I don't think anyone knows, or they're just not telling us."

"Has the religion always been worshiped?"

"Yes, but about two hundred years ago, they went from an obscure religion to one that controlled the city."

Cullen nodded slowly. "Do you know why?"

"They might have told me, but I never paid attention. Even before I felt my magic, something deep within me warned that the religion was wrong. Any sort of belief that teaches sacrifice and intolerance should be eradicated."

"I agree, but we are no' here to wipe out those philosophies. We're here to save children."

She gawked at him. "How long do you think that will work? They'll keep finding children with magic and killing them long after you and I are gone."

"I'm no' disagreeing with you. What I'm saying is that right now, we focus on saving those we can. In the meantime, what you want needs to be done slowly. Things as they are didna happen overnight. They took time. It'll take time to unravel them."

Tamlyn knew he was right. Why then did her stomach clench in dread? She had the distinct feeling that time wasn't on their side.

"Tell me about the soldiers," Cullen said, breaking into her thoughts.

She shrugged. "Children are tested very young on certain skills. That's how they're put into different classifications regarding what they'll learn to do in order to pull their weight in the city."

"No one gets to choose their job?"

"No," she said with a shake of her head. "Some children are chosen early and put into the army to become ruthless and merciless, upholding the laws of Stonemore without question."

Cullen quirked a brow. "Is Stonemore often in clashes with other cities or villages?"

"They send out battalions sometimes, but I have no idea where they go or what they do. There used to be a few villages within a day's walk of Stonemore. There's nothing left of them now."

"You think the army did this?"

She shrugged and shook her head. "I can tell you the city is overcrowded."

"People probably remain because they feel safe."

"They're terrified of anyone with magic. Stonemore promises to eradicate anyone who has it."

Cullen twisted his lips. "The priests have done their job well."

Tamlyn sighed and looked upward at the tower. "I know the way things are is wrong. I feel as if I have an obligation to not only save innocent children but also change the minds of those who fear us."

"I think your first step is learning why everyone is so terrified of magic. I have a suspicion it starts with the dragons."

Her head lowered to look into his pale brown eyes. "Why did you come back today?"

"I told you."

"You could have gone to Stonemore yourself. You don't need me. You're a Dragon King."

Cullen shrugged one shoulder. "I've been alive for so many millennia, I've lost count. I've seen civilizations rise and fall, religions come out of obscurity and topple those that were in place for thousands of years. I've seen so many wars, it's a wonder any humans are left to populate my realm. I've fought wars with other magical beings the mortals knew nothing about, all to keep Earth safe. Each Dragon King is powerful in his own right, but when we fight together, we're unstoppable. Aye, I can do this on my own. But I'm choosing to partner with you because of your dedication and knowledge."

"Oh," she murmured.

"I promised I wouldna start a war. That's important to both sides. The information you give me will help me prevent just that."

She nodded, slightly disappointed that she hadn't been the reason he returned. It was silly. He had only seen her for a short time that morning. What could she possibly have that a Dragon King would be interested in?

"I couldna stop thinking about you."

Her gaze jerked to him. "What?"

"I saw something on your face this morning as you and the lad ran from the soldiers. You were scared, aye, but there was such determination there. You were no' going to give up."

"I can't," she whispered.

One side of his lips lifted in a quick grin. "I know. You have a gift. What you and your friends have created is extraordinary. I want to help you succeed while also completing my mission."

Tamlyn didn't know what to say. No one had complimented her in a while. Not that Jenefer and Sian didn't appreciate her. She knew they did. But they had been together for so long that none of them said it anymore. Maybe that was the problem. Just because they appreciated each other didn't mean they shouldn't continue saying it.

She swallowed, now self-conscious. "I think your best bet is to look in Stonemore for your enemy. Anyone who would dare to kill dragons will most likely be there with other magic-haters."

"I'm no' so sure. Magic killed the dragons and wounded others."

"That means you're looking for those with magic."

Chapter Twelve

Long after Tamlyn left him, her last words turned over in his head again and again. He sat on the floor in the dark, leaning against a wall in his chamber with his knees up and his arms resting atop them. There had been disappointment and resignation in her gaze, but that wasn't to be helped. She wasn't the one attacking the dragons. However, he was going to find out who it was and put an end to it.

He understood why Brandr and Eurwen kept the humans to their lands so they didn't interfere with the dragons' lives, but the mortals with magic were stuck in the middle. The humans didn't want them because of their abilities, and the dragons didn't want them because they were human. It seemed to Cullen that if any group could get along, it was the dragons and the magic-bearing humans.

It was a long shot to be sure. But someone had to try. If things continued as they were, there would be a war. Those with magic would only take so much before they turned to the only weapon they had—their powers—and used them on the humans. After the mortals had ruthlessly hunted and relentlessly killed those with magic, Cullen couldn't blame them.

The humans had been in power for a long time, but the tides were slowly shifting to those with magic. The mortals wouldn't see it until it was too late. Then the persecuted and oppressed would take their vengeance. It would be a slaughter.

Based on what Cullen had learned from Jeyra and Varek, as well as Tamlyn and her friends, the humans deserved everything they had coming. That didn't mean he liked the idea of it. He would never understand why people couldn't be more tolerant, more accepting. Just because someone was different didn't make them evil or wrong. It just made them different.

He sighed and got to his feet. He was restless. He tried to tell himself it was because he was impatient to see Stonemore for himself, but it had nothing to do with that. It was about Tamlyn and their kiss.

Unable to help himself, he touched his lips. He could still taste her desire, feel the need that had rushed through her. Hear her ragged breaths. He'd wanted to claim her body right then, but somehow, he had gotten control of himself and ended the kiss. The way she'd responded to his kiss told him that she'd wanted it as much as he did, but when she jumped away from him, it had hurt him—though he wished he could deny it.

He ran a hand down his face in frustration. What he needed was a cold shower.

Instead, he walked from the chamber. Cullen had no destination in mind other than to explore more of the ruin complex. He found more corridors, rooms, and other courtyards, but nothing came close to the first one. It wasn't magic but science that shed the light through the patios, but that didn't make it any less stunning.

When he first came to the ruins, he'd thought it might be an ancient city for those with magic. There was no evidence of that except for possibly the stone. He hadn't investigated that too much since his attention was on other things, but the stone had probably been mined from somewhere on Zora.

Somehow, Cullen wasn't surprised when he ended up back in the great hall. At least that was what he called it. It was grand, and it was similar to the halls from castles. He walked to the pool and looked up at the tangle of roots. Some were no larger than his arm. Others, he wasn't sure he could get his arms around.

He was awed by the way they had disrupted the architecture by pulling apart some of the stones. Yet it was the root system that now supported the temple. To become a stunning work of nature that complemented the ruins instead of distracting from them.

Cullen lowered his gaze to the water and waited. Jenefer had been following him for some time. He didn't alert her to give her a chance to see that he was an ally. He understood the Amazon's wounded pride. She was their protector, and he had stepped on her toes. Cullen was used to working with other alphas, but he hadn't taken into consideration that

Jenefer wasn't.

"You can come out of the shadows," he said as he turned his head toward her.

She moved out of the darkness of a hallway beneath the flickering light of a torch.

He turned to face her. "If I wanted to harm anyone here, I could've already done it."

"You expect us to trust you so easily?"

"Trust has to be earned."

Jenefer walked closer and stopped about six feet away. "Tamlyn is willing to put her life in your hands."

"But you willna?"

"She isn't thinking straight. She sees a Dragon King who wants to help. What she sees is someone who can do what she's been unable to do."

Cullen asked, "What's that?"

"Save all of us."

He shook his head. "To do that would mean war."

"You've known Tamlyn a few hours. We've known her for years. We've sat with her when she was unable to locate one of the children from her visions. We know how she suffers after. We know how she puts her life at risk to rescue each kid." Anger rolled from Jenefer. "You give her false hope."

"I doona. I told her I can help, and I shall."

"For how long?" she snapped. "A week? A month? Do you think this ends for us then? It will never end as long as we're persecuted and exiled."

Cullen drew in a slow breath. "I doona know how long I'll be here. I've not made any promises other than I'll not instigate a war."

"It would've been better had we never met you."

He opened his mouth to respond when Sian shouted Jenefer's name as she came running into the hall, out of breath. Cullen spun to the petite Alchemist, but her gaze was on her lover.

"She's gone," Sian said, her face lined with fear.

Cullen took a step toward her. "Who?"

"Tamlyn," Jenefer said as she strode past him. To Sian, she said, "Stay here. If the dragon's right, this place is protected. You know where to take the children."

He rolled his eyes. "You are protected."

"Find her," Sian said, ignoring him. "After this morning, this is definitely a trap."

Cullen made his way to the women. He looked at Sian first. "You and the kids are safe, but take them to a secure location in the complex if you have it." Then he turned his head to Jenefer. "I'm going after Tamlyn. Will you work with me so we can bring her back?"

"Jenefer," Sian admonished when the Amazon hesitated.

Jenefer's nostrils flared. "Fine. Yes, I'll work with you."

Cullen headed toward the main entrance when Sian called his name. When he turned, he saw Jenefer walking the other way. He held back his retort and ran to catch up with her. He was the outsider here, and while he had some advantages that could aid them, that didn't mean they couldn't do without him.

"Keep up," Jenefer snapped.

He didn't bother to tell her that she would be the one trying to keep up with him. "Where are you going?"

"Tamlyn found another exit about six months ago. It's faster than climbing up the canyon."

What she didn't tell him was that it meant running through a maze of corridors before climbing stairs that never seemed to end. Cullen thought that Jenefer was leading him in the wrong direction at first, but they soon arrived back where they should, with the ground sloping upward. Then, finally, a doorway nearly covered with tree roots appeared. Jenefer wiggled through the roots first. Cullen followed to find her waiting for him.

"There's a main path in the forest. It's the easiest and quickest way to go," she said and glanced at the woods ahead of them. "The soldiers will be waiting for her there. That means we have to go through the forest."

Something in her voice alerted him. "Is there something I should know about the woods?"

"Be quiet. Don't let anything hear you."

"We doona have time for that if we're to catch up with Tamlyn."

Jenefer's lips pressed together. "If we want to survive, we don't have a choice."

Cullen wasn't going to sit around and talk about it. He started running. Jenefer caught up with him as they ran side by side.

"If she doesn't get to save the child, things will be bad," the Amazon said.

He met her gaze and nodded. There wasn't time to discover exactly what she meant. If Jenefer didn't get to Tamlyn, he would. He was certain of that. His gaze locked on the dark woods ahead. They looked no different than the forests on Earth, but he wasn't stupid, either. He would take Jenefer's caution to heart.

Cullen fought not to pull ahead of her. He wanted to shift and take to the sky to find Tamlyn, but he had to curb that need quickly, or the promises he'd made would be broken on the first night.

The instant Jenefer was inside the woods, she came to a halt. Cullen fisted his hands in frustration as he stopped with her. The forest was dense with trees and the sea of deep green plant life on the ground. His enhanced hearing picked up various animal sounds through the many layers of the woods.

She pointed to the right to show him where the road lay. He moved his gaze deeper into the forest and spotted the hidden men—three on either side of the road. He motioned to her, and Jenefer nodded that she saw them.

She began moving through the woods. Cullen gnashed his teeth at their slow pace. As they drew even with the soldiers, he noted how nervous they looked. Their attention wasn't strictly on the road. He and Jenefer were about a hundred yards from them, but they kept looking around as if searching for something. Cullen squatted and yanked Jenefer down beside him just as a soldier looked their way.

A roar that sounded like a big cat filled the silence.

"Shite," Jenefer mumbled.

Cullen looked at her and shrugged in question.

Her lips flattened before she whispered, "It's a wildcat. Not something you want to encounter."

Cullen looked at the warriors once more. When he turned back to Jenefer, she was gone. He caught sight of her ahead of him. He straightened and stealthily followed her. They didn't so much as move a leaf as they passed.

The deeper into the forest they went, the harder it became. They passed two more sets of soldiers waiting for Tamlyn. The wildcat roared again, this time closer. Cullen hoped they were following Tamlyn. If she was on the other side of the road, then that could make things difficult.

He looked ahead as Jenefer tried to navigate a tight spot. Cullen spotted the army waiting for them. He touched Jenefer's arm and pointed. She sucked in a breath and stilled. Both frantically searched for some sign of Tamlyn, but there was nothing. If the army already had her, they wouldn't still be waiting. Cullen didn't know the forest or the people. He felt helpless, and it wasn't something he was familiar with. Nor did he like it.

Another roar, even closer, had him looking to his right. He heard some soldiers shout as they caught sight of the animal. Cullen saw the black fur through the foliage as it chased something. He looked ahead and locked his gaze on Tamlyn.

The cat gained on her quickly. She had no place to go. The animal was behind her, warriors to her right, and an army ahead. Cullen had to make a quick decision. There wasn't time to tell Jenefer anything.

He called up his power. Opaque fog poured from his mouth and quickly filled the area, spreading through the forest. Then, he headed for Tamlyn.

Chapter Thirteen

The instant she saw the fog, Tamlyn stopped. She knew this was Cullen. She wanted to look for him, but the mist was too thick. Thankfully, it had also slowed the wildcat.

She swallowed, the sound loud to her ears. The forest had gone deathly quiet when the fog appeared. Even the wildcat's roars had ceased. Her head snapped to the side when she heard a man's voice. It was some distance away and was quickly followed by another's. Those must be the soldiers waiting for her again.

Tamlyn's chest rose and fell rapidly. She didn't have time for this. She had to get to the temple. Her hands were sweaty. She rubbed them on her hips and took a step. As she moved forward, a limb snapped beneath her foot. She stilled once more. It felt as if every eye in the forest was looking at her.

The soldiers began talking again. She couldn't make out what they were saying, but it couldn't be good. They were there for her. She had barely made it back yesterday morning. Tamlyn shook her head, refusing to let her thoughts go down that road. Suddenly, an arm came around her waist as a hand covered her mouth. She found herself pressed against a firm chest. She fought with all she had.

"Lass, it's me."

At the sound of Cullen's voice, her body went limp. She removed his hand from her mouth and turned in his arms. He put a finger to his lips and shook his head. She didn't know how he had found her, and she didn't care. He was there now.

She took his hand and tried to tug him after her, but he refused to budge. Tamlyn faced him once more and shot him a look of outrage.

A muscle ticked in his jaw as the mist hovered around them. He leaned close and put his mouth against her ear. "There's an army waiting for you, spread the length of the forest."

She jerked back. Her heart plummeted to her feet as she shook her head. That couldn't be.

Cullen nodded once.

Tamlyn looked around, hoping that the answer to her problem would suddenly appear. Her gaze kept returning to Cullen. He couldn't be her answer. He was the one preventing her from going. He didn't understand that to not at least try to find the child about to die would be akin to feeling the blade herself.

She released his hand and spun around. Two steps later, he had his arms wrapped around her again.

"You can no'," he murmured near her ear.

Tears poured down her face as the screams rang out in her head. A picture of a little girl's face filled her mind. The child was barely four with chubby cheeks and an easy smile. Tamlyn fought to get free of Cullen, but his hold was firm.

"Please," she begged. "I have to go. Let me go before it's too late."

She didn't care if the entire realm heard her. Nothing was worse than not being able to do something to save the child.

Cullen didn't release her. Tamlyn struggled in his arms, kicking and flailing to no avail. She threw back her head. Pain exploded as she connected with his. He mumbled a curse but held tight, his arms locking around her.

She didn't give up the fight. Then, suddenly, somehow, she managed to get free. Tamlyn ran through the forest as fast as she could. She could make it to the city. She could save the little girl. If only she could get to the—

"Enough!" Cullen hissed in her ear as he caught her once more. "You're running to your death."

The screams in her head grew louder. Tamlyn clawed at her face, trying to hush them. A picture of the little girl flashed in her mind again. This time, the child was crying, fear causing her little body to shake.

And just as suddenly as it all began, it ended.

The agony within her was so great, it was all she could feel…all she could be. She wanted to…she didn't know what she needed. It was there, just out of reach. She tried to grab it, but it slipped through her fingers.

* * * *

"Tamlyn?" Cullen whispered when she went slack in his arms.

Her eyes were closed, and she wasn't breathing.

"Tamlyn, breathe," he ordered. When she didn't respond, he knelt and shook her once more. "Breathe, dammit."

Jenefer ran to him, out of breath with her sword drawn, blood coating it. She took one look at Tamlyn and dropped down beside him. "Shite. Shite."

"What do I do?" he asked in a hushed tone.

She looked helplessly at him and shrugged. "There's nothing to do."

"There has to be."

"She'll come out of it. At least she has in the past."

That didn't make Cullen feel any better. He shook Tamlyn again, this time harder, but she didn't so much as blink.

"Uh. I think we have a problem, dragon."

He looked up to find Jenefer staring at the face of a large cat, its green gaze locked on them, its mouth slightly parted showing rows of razor-sharp teeth. It had black fur with gray spots and rosettes. By his guess, the feline was about five hundred pounds of hungry beast. Fortunately, there was plenty for it to eat elsewhere in the forest. Cullen could kill the cat easily, but he didn't want to. It was just doing what it did. They were in *its* territory.

Cullen looked deep into the animal's eyes, showing it who he really was. The wildcat blinked its green orbs and sat back. It hadn't run off as most animals did when he looked them in the eye in such a way. He smiled as understanding dawned. The cat was intelligent. Cullen motioned to the army behind them. The feline stood and cut its gaze to Jenefer before trotting around Cullen to disappear into the fog.

"What the hell?" Jenefer asked.

Cullen shrugged at the same time screams filled the air—the army's. He looked down at Tamlyn and shook her. She jerked without opening her eyes but let out a scream that was drowned out by the men's. Then, she fell unconscious.

"Let's get her back to the ruins," he said.

He stood and lifted her in his arms. With the cat enjoying its dinner, and the army otherwise occupied, they ran to the road and then straight through the forest to the canyon. Jenefer didn't fall that far behind him.

When they entered the ruins, Jenefer went ahead of him and motioned for him to follow her. "Sian," Jenefer called as they hurried through the corridors.

Cullen found himself in a chamber with a pallet of furs on the floor for a bed. He gently laid Tamlyn down.

"No," Sian said as she came into the room.

He quickly got out of the way and let Jenefer and Sian do what they could. For the second time that night, he felt powerless. It was an emotion he was coming to detest greatly. He'd be happy to never feel it again. Unfortunately, he wasn't sure he had that option.

"She screamed," Jenefer said.

Sian didn't pause as she felt Tamlyn's forehead. "What?"

"She screamed," Jenefer repeated.

Sian sat back after a few moments. "Her breathing has finally evened out. She should be fine in a few hours." She took a deep breath and then released it. "Tam has never screamed before."

"She said she hears the screams in her head," Cullen said.

Jenefer nodded. "That's right."

"We have myths on my realm about Banshees, but they're the ones who scream. If you hear their scream, it means you or someone in your family is about to die."

Sian shrugged and looked between them. "I know what Tamlyn tells us. I've never met another Banshee, so I don't know if this is supposed to happen or not."

"It's not," Jenefer said in a hard tone. "It can't. One of these days, she's not going to breathe again." The Amazon got to her feet and paced the chamber. "I told her to find me the next time. She promised she would. She promised she wouldn't go by herself."

Sian stood and ushered them out, saying in a low voice, "Something woke me. I don't know what it was, but it could have been Tamlyn shouting for you. I got up, and when you weren't in bed, I decided to check on Tam. That's when I found her gone."

"There was an army waiting for her," Cullen said as they walked down the hallway to the kitchen and sat at the table.

Sian's face paled. "She would've died tonight."

"She nearly did anyway. A wildcat was after her," Jenefer said. She looked across the table at Cullen. "What did you do to the animal?"

"I showed it what I was," he explained.

Sian's brows lifted. "What happened?"

Cullen twisted his lips. "Oddly, it didna run off. It sat there and looked at me. Then I reminded it that others were in the forest."

"It turned the army's attention from us," Jenefer said with a small smile.

But it faded quickly. No doubt she was thinking about Tamlyn, just as Cullen was.

* * * *

Tamlyn woke to a horrible headache. She put her hand to her forehead and winced. There would be no more sleep for her until it abated. Memories of what'd happened filled her. They weren't as stark or unforgiving as before, but the pain was still fresh. Raw.

Tears filled her eyes. They fell down her temples and into her hair. The agony from the child's death would stay with her for some time. It didn't matter how many she saved; it never lightened the load of the dead that she carried with her.

She sat up and drew her knees to her chest. Much about the end of the night was fuzzy, but she did remember Cullen being there. He'd tried to stop her and had warned her about an army. An *army*!

If he hadn't been there, she would've been captured. A shiver raced down her spine as she imagined what the priests would have done to her as punishment for meddling with their so-called sacrifices. It wouldn't matter what torture they put her through. Nothing was worse than not saving a child and having to live with that.

"You were supposed to get me."

Tamlyn lifted her head to find Jenefer in the doorway. "I called out for you several times."

"You should've waited."

"I couldn't. You know that."

Jenefer sighed. "It's a good thing Sian woke up and checked on you. I'm beginning to think you shouldn't sleep alone."

Her thoughts immediately went to Cullen. Tamlyn looked away from Jenefer so her friend couldn't see her thoughts.

"You really scared us tonight, Tam."

She looked into Jenefer's brown eyes and gave her a woeful smile. "I'm sorry."

"I know," Jenefer said with a sad smile before walking away.

Tamlyn wouldn't be able to sleep until she had taken something for her head. She rose and went to Sian's lab to look for the vial of purple liquid. It was a concoction Sian had made specifically for Tamlyn and the headaches that assaulted her after failing to reach a child.

It tasted vile, but it worked. Tamlyn scrunched up her nose and took a big swig of it. She gagged and forced herself to swallow. She gagged a second time and rushed to a bucket in case it came up. After Tamlyn was sure that it would stay down, she straightened and turned around, only to find herself staring into pale brown eyes.

"How are you feeling?"

She shrugged and returned the vial to its rightful place. "I'll be better once that kicks in and takes away the headache."

"Was it from the headbutt you gave me?" Cullen asked with a grin.

Tamlyn bit her lip as his words triggered her memory. "No, but I'm really sorry about that. When I hear the screams, I have no choice but to go."

"I found that out tonight."

"I would've been caught if it hadn't been for you."

He quirked a blond brow. "It doesna make your unsuccessful rescue easier to bear, does it?"

"No."

Cullen pushed away from the door and walked into the lab. "I've been doing some thinking while you slept. The soldiers know you come through the forest."

"But they don't know who I am."

He waved away her words. "That isna what I mean. When you hear the screams, you have to run the length of the forest to get to the temple and free the children. Then you have to make your way back through the woods, as well as past whatever animals or soldiers might be waiting."

"Yes," she said, wondering what he was getting at.

"There's a way we can get around that."

Tamlyn forced a smile. "We've thought of everything."

"You have no' thought of already being in the city."

"You're serious?"

He smiled and turned on his heel. As he walked away, he said, "I told you I was going to the city, lass."

Chapter Fourteen

"It's insane," Tamlyn said for the third time that morning.

Cullen stood in the great hall, watching the three women. To his surprise, Jenefer had agreed with his plan to go to Stonemore.

"This'd better work," Sian stated, her eyes on him.

"It will." Cullen understood her uncertainty. They barely knew him, and he wanted to go into a place they feared and hated. He could point out that he wasn't forcing Tamlyn to accompany him. But he decided it would be better to keep that to himself.

Tamlyn pursed her lips and blew out a breath. Her nervousness was palpable. "What if they recognize me?"

"They won't," Jenefer said. "You were a child when you escaped."

Cullen briefly met Jenefer's gaze. "She's right. You have nothing to worry about."

"That's easy for you to say," Tamlyn mumbled.

Sian embraced Tamlyn, squeezing her tightly. "It's only for a little while. We'll be waiting for your return." Sian stepped back and locked her eyes on Cullen. "She *will* be back."

"Aye, she will," he replied.

Jenefer smiled to Tamlyn as she moved to stand before her. "You've been in and out of that city multiple times. They didn't get you then, and they won't now."

Tamlyn nodded before hugging Jenefer.

The Amazon quickly released her and stepped back. "You two should go. No need to tarry."

Tamlyn looked pointedly at Cullen's outfit.

He remembered the clothes she had described to him yesterday. Using his magic, he called brown pants made of the same material as Tamlyn's and chose a darker brown for his shirt. When he looked up, he found Tamlyn staring at him. He glanced down to see that the deep V of the shirt showed off a large portion of his chest. Good. He wanted her to look. To feel the same fire that burned within him.

Because he couldn't take his eyes off her.

He nodded to Jenefer and Sian, both looking a little awed at his display of magic, as he passed. When he came even with Tamlyn, his head swung to her. She took a deep breath and turned to head up the steps and out the door. Just before she stepped through, Tamlyn lingered and looked back at her friends. She lifted a hand in a wave, a small smile playing about her lips.

He paused at the top of the steps and looked over his shoulder. Jenefer had already walked away, but Sian remained, doubt and worry clouding her face. Cullen nodded to her before continuing after Tamlyn. The longer he was with these women, the more infuriated he became on their behalf. They were formidable in their own right, but they had been told from a young age that there was something wrong with them for having magic. That they were worthless. Powerless.

His promise not to start a war might be more difficult than he imagined. As a magical being, he had a responsibility not to use his powers for evil. Yet, the humans were doing that with their words and actions. All because of their fear and tiny, tiny minds.

Cullen fell into step with Tamlyn as they began climbing out of the canyon. "I wouldna take you with me if I didna think I could protect you."

"I know you think that, but you don't know Stonemore."

He frowned as she used her hands to pull herself up over a steep part. "These people doona have magic. They have nothing to prevent me from safeguarding both of us and getting us out."

"Without starting a war?" she asked without looking at him.

He sighed. "You know I fly get us to the top of the canyon in a blink."

"I've climbed the canyon many times."

Cullen let the matter drop, but he stayed near her just in case. A few minutes later, the rock she gripped loosened and fell. He easily reached out with his free hand and caught her as she started to fall, yanking her to him.

The instant she was flush with his body, his gaze dropped to her lips. Memories of the previous day, of her lips against his, her softness yielding to him, *seeking* him, made his blood pound in his ears. It felt good to have her pressed against him. Her heat against him made him hold her tighter.

She gasped as she gripped him. "Th-thank you."

"I'm no' the enemy, lass." He barely got the words out. His desire had risen quickly. Her nearness made him forget everything but her.

Tamlyn lowered her eyes as she sighed. "I know. I'm sorry. I just hate Stonemore so much."

"You doona have to go."

"I do." Her hazel eyes lifted to his.

For a long moment, they silently stared at each other. He wanted to know what was going through her mind. Because thoughts of her filled his. Cullen knew the best thing for him was to return to dragon land and send someone else in his stead, but he couldn't. Whatever it was about Tamlyn that had him contemplating ignoring a direct order from Con kept him with her now.

"Are we going to hang here all day?" A slow smile spread over her face.

Cullen realized that both of their feet were dangling. His grip with his other hand kept them from falling. He said nothing as he moved her closer to the side of the cliff so she could find her foot and handholds. He didn't release her until she was settled. The rest of the climb was uneventful.

At the top, he dusted off his hands and looked around. His gaze moved through the invisible barrier that kept the humans from dragon land. He spotted a dragon in the distance and could just make out gold scales. He assumed it was Brandr since he was supposed to take Cullen's place. But it could be Con.

Cullen hadn't checked in with Con or any of the others since he had left dragon land. He would need to soon. Once he and Tamlyn were in the city, he would let them know his progress.

"You can go back."

He jerked his head to Tamlyn and frowned. "What?"

"You're staring at your land."

"Dragon land," he corrected.

She shot him a flat look. "You know what I mean."

"Do you see the dragon in the distance?"

Tamlyn looked to where he pointed. She squinted, her gaze moving over the sky. Finally, she shook her head. "Can you?"

"Aye."

"Like I said, you can go back."

He started toward Ferdon Woods, ignoring her words. When she jogged to catch up with him, he said, "For too long, I've no' been able to see dragons in the sky. It's nice to see them flying whenever they want."

"And nice for you to fly whenever *you* want."

He looked at her and smiled. "Verra much."

"Does it hurt?"

"What?"

"When you shift from dragon to human and back?"

He shrugged. "The first time was excruciating. It's a good thing none of us tried to run or fight right after because we were clumsy." He laughed at the memory. "We had no idea how to use our arms or legs. Our wings and tails were suddenly gone. It was verra…strange."

"I can imagine," she said with a chuckle.

"The shift happens so quickly, that we doona feel anything. Or perhaps we doona allow ourselves to think about it."

"Or maybe your bodies are used to it now."

He grinned. "Maybe."

Her smile faded as she stared at the approaching forest. "I can't remember the last time I walked into the woods like this."

"No one will be looking for you today."

"What if there are soldiers?"

"Let me take care of it."

She focused on the forest so hard that Cullen feared she would crack. He had to take her mind off it because if she was like this with the woods, she would be worse at Stonemore.

"Does everyone speak the same language here?" he asked.

Tamlyn glanced at him sharply as if she were annoyed to have her thoughts interrupted. "What?"

"Your dialect. We call it English. Does everyone speak it?"

She shook her head. "We call it Urtish."

"Urtish," he said, trying out the name.

"Other languages are spoken. There's Surun and Istrati, that I know of. I've heard there are others, but I've not traveled that far to hear them."

"Can you speak Surun or Istrati?"

She wrinkled her nose. "Not very well. The Surun language is that of the Amazons. Jenefer taught me some of it. I can understand it if spoken, but I can't really make myself understood."

"And the Istrati?"

"A little." She said a phrase that sounded like a cross between those spoken in Asia and India.

He motioned for her to say more. She repeated the sentence. By the middle of it, he understood what she was saying and replied to her in the same language.

Tamlyn halted, her eyes wide. "You know Istrati?"

"I do now."

"You can pick up languages like that?"

He nodded, smiling. "All Dragon Kings can."

"Well, that should make things easy for you."

They continued onward. Cullen wondered if she'd realized they had just entered the woods. He wasn't going to tell her. She was relaxed, her mind on other things.

"How many languages does your realm have?" she asked.

Cullen made a face. "Over six thousand."

"That many? How many people are there?"

"Over seven billion."

Her gaze locked on the dirt road as she absorbed that. "I can't fathom that number."

"Do you know how many are on Zora?"

"Not a clue," she said as she briefly met his gaze. Then she looked around, comprehending where she was. She swung her head back to him, but there was no censure on her face as she smiled. "Thank you for distracting me."

"I willna let anything happen to you."

She twisted her lips and looked farther down the winding road. "I'm not sure I can make that same promise."

Cullen laughed softly. "I'll be fine, lass."

"You have a peculiar accent."

"It's called Scottish where I'm from."

"Is Urtish, I mean…what did you call this language?"

"English," he offered.

She nodded. "Is English your main language?"

"In this form."

Her brows shot up in her forehead. "What language do dragons speak?"

"We communicate telepathically. Meaning, we doona use words with our mouths, but with our minds."

"That's amazing," she replied softly.

Cullen was pleased at the astonishment that brightened her eyes. "What else do you want to know?"

Chapter Fifteen

What did she want to know? Everything, of course.

Tamlyn decided not to say that. However, if he offered, she wouldn't let the chance pass her by. "The place you live is Dreagan?"

"That's the home of the Dragon Kings, aye," he answered, walking casually.

She tried to mimic his relaxed attitude, but her gaze darted around, looking for any of the dangerous animals that could show up during the day. They preferred the night, but that wouldn't stop them if they were hungry. "Is it big?"

"Sixty thousand acres."

Tamlyn laughed. "I'd definitely say that's big."

"The country where Dreagan is located is called Scotland. It's an island. We share it with another country, England."

She smiled wistfully. "I've only ever seen a lake. I know Zora has oceans, but I've never seen one."

"Is it that you're too afraid to venture from here?"

"That's partly it. Sian doesn't want to go too far from her twin."

"How far is Mair?"

"Three days south."

"It's been a long time since Sian escaped. Is she sure her sister is still alive?"

Tamlyn shrugged. "We don't know."

"How long are you going to wait to free her?"

She glanced at him. "We've come up with different plans, but they won't work."

"Why no'?"

"The moment anyone sees Jenefer, they'll know exactly what she is."

"Is there no' other tall women?"

Tamlyn shook her head. "Everyone knows Sian's face since her sister is an identical twin, so she can't go."

"And you doona have defensive magic to use."

"Precisely."

He was silent for a few moments. "What's the other reason you've no' left?"

"Fear of what we might encounter."

"Better the enemy you know," he mumbled.

She frowned at him. "What?"

"Nothing," he said with a shake of his head. "I'm no' promising anything, but I might be able to help with Sian's sister."

Tamlyn had known he would offer. She didn't know Cullen well, but she had learned quickly enough that he wanted to help those he deemed in need. There was no doubt that she and her friends were desperately in need. "That's kind of you, but it isn't necessary."

"Do you no' want my help?"

She looked at him when she heard the hurt in his voice. He refused to look at her, leaving her no choice but to be blunt. "Aiding me in rescuing children about to be sacrificed is far different than freeing Sian's twin."

"How so?"

"Mair is a slave. They watched her and Sian constantly before Sian escaped. Things will have only gotten worse. Getting to the home of the couple holding Mair will be impossible. They fear anyone taking their Alchemist. But all of that is a moot point because we'd never get out of the city if we managed to get Mair."

Cullen cut his gaze to her. "We could fly out."

A laugh burst from Tamlyn. "So much for not alerting anyone to our presence."

"Too much, huh?" he asked.

She nodded, chuckling at his fake seriousness. "You could say that."

"Let's concentrate on our current mission, but I'm no' finished asking about Mair."

"Just don't say anything in front of Sian. She gets very low every time she's reminded that her sister is still being held."

"Understood."

She glanced at him. "What does Scotland look like?"

"Heaven," he replied immediately, a smile curving his lips. He got a faraway look in his eyes. "The weather is as unpredictable and wild as the terrain. Craggy mountains rise to the sky with glens of vibrant green between. The lochs are numerous, as are the waterfalls. Some might call it inhospitable, but I love the stark beauty."

He painted a beautiful picture, but she wasn't sure of some words. "Glens?"

"Valleys," he explained.

"Lochs?"

"Lakes."

"Ah," she said as that made sense. "I'd like to see your Scotland."

A hint of sadness touched his face. "You should've seen it before most of the forests were cut down. I've seen a lot of beautiful places, but Scotland will always hold my heart."

"I've never felt that about any place. I've always just wanted to hide and feel safe."

His blond head swiveled to her. "We'll find you a place."

It was wishful thinking, but right now she needed some of that.

When she looked forward, she spotted a group of soldiers ahead.

"Easy," Cullen whispered. "Let me handle it."

The sight of the soldiers reminded her of the previous night and how close she had come to being captured. She was thankful that Cullen wanted to speak because she wasn't sure she would be able to. Her entire body shook. And she was sure that everyone could see it.

Cullen's hand found hers and lightly squeezed it. The action calmed her somewhat. She thought he might release her, but when he didn't, she twined her fingers with his. Something about holding his hand felt comforting and...right.

She didn't dare look at him, though she desperately wanted to. His conviction and certainty gave her the courage she needed to enter Ferdon Woods. His confidence wasn't shaken as they stopped in front of the soldiers, and she hoped she could be the same.

The men looked them over. The one closest to her walked behind her. She started to turn to look at him, but Cullen's fingers tightened on hers. She tried to listen to what the soldier asked, but the other three staring at her broke her attention. They couldn't know who she was, or even recognize her. Yet she couldn't help but think that they could. She would never have walked the road and chanced being stopped by the soldiers. She had tried to warn Cullen. Now, they would be detained and possibly imprisoned. She had to do something. Didn't Cullen understand that the soldiers might not have magic, but they had ways to—

"Thank you," Cullen said in an accent that perfectly mimicked hers, then he yanked her.

She blinked, trying to hide her shock as the soldiers moved out of the way and allowed them to continue. Disbelief slowly ran through her, her knees threatening to buckle with each step.

"I told you it would be fine," Cullen murmured.

"Are they following?"

"Nay."

She glanced at him, swallowing hard. "Are you sure?"

"I doona hear them."

They went a little farther before Cullen asked, "What happened back there? You looked like you were about to bolt."

"I thought they knew who I was," she whispered.

He sighed, his frustration clear. "They can no'."

"You've not lived my life. You have no idea what I've endured," she said angrily.

His thumb moved over the back of her hand. Tamlyn peevishly yanked her hand away. The moment she did, she regretted it. She'd liked having that contact with him. It was because of his hand on hers that she hadn't given in to her anxiety with the soldiers. As much as she bemoaned pulling her hand away, she didn't reach for his again. Her pride prevented it.

No matter what he might think, she had done the best she could. He was frustrated because she didn't fall at his feet and take every word he said as truth. He had no idea what it was to truly fear. And nothing she said would remedy that.

They walked the rest of the forest in silence. Tamlyn felt his gaze on her several times, but she didn't look his way. He made her feel as if her anxieties and concerns meant nothing—right after she had begun to warm to him. She hadn't expected it from Cullen, which made it worse.

Right before they came to the edge of the forest, Cullen reached out and brought her to a halt. He faced her, and while Tamlyn wanted to ignore him, it was childish. His brown eyes held hers as if searching for something.

"I'm sorry I upset you."

There was sincerity in his words and his voice. She glanced away, taken aback by him once more.

"It's wrong to expect you to hand all your trust over at once." He shot her a charming smile. "Forgive me?"

Damn him for being so persuasive. "Yes."

His smile crinkled the corners of his eyes as he flashed white teeth. "I'll no' make the same mistake twice."

All her anger vanished, and she wasn't certain she liked that. How could he infuriate her so quickly, and just as swiftly, snatch it away? Not that she held grudges, but she had worked herself up on their walk. His apology had taken the fuel from her fire, leaving her with nothing.

He glanced at the city through the trees. "Ready?"

"No," she answered honestly. "I hate this place."

"I bet a lot of people do, but they doona think they have another choice. Their fear locks them in place."

She narrowed her gaze at him. "You think mine has locked me to this area?"

"It's possible. Frankly, I'm glad of it because I got to meet you."

A smile curved her lips, the last vestiges of her anger fading with his comment. Her gaze briefly lowered to his mouth as she thought of their kiss the day before.

"I'm serious," he said, holding her gaze.

"You might come to regret saying that."

He chuckled, shaking his head. "Nay, lass. I willna."

She turned her head to stare at the gates into the city. Trepidation filled her. She would never attempt this on her own, or even with Sian or Jenefer. Only Cullen could talk her into such a daring feat.

"You can do it. You got through the forest and the encounter with the soldiers," he said.

Tamlyn glanced at him and squared her shoulders. "I'd rather be here if a child needs to be rescued. It'll save time. It's just that I know what kind of evil resides within the walls."

"No harm will come to you. I swear it."

The fervor in his tone caused her to look at him. "I believe you."

"Then walk into the city as if you own it."

He gave her a nod, and she returned it. Then they faced the city together. To her delight, Cullen reached for her hand again.

Chapter Sixteen

Before Cullen walked from the woods, his gaze scanned the top of the wall that ran from the mountain on the right and then curved to encompass the city before ending at the mountain on the left. The steep mountainside made it nearly impossible for a mortal to climb down to the city. That ensured the only way in and out was through the gates.

"What?" Tamlyn asked as they emerged from the forest.

"I was just thinking how the builders thought they were clever in how they designed the city to keep others out."

She glanced at him. "They weren't thinking about dragons."

"No' just dragons. Fae and Warriors could get in easily."

Her head jerked to him. "Warriors?"

"No' the kind you're used to. These are skilled men and a woman who have primeval gods within them, allowing them special powers and abilities."

"Are they your friends?"

"Aye."

She nodded and faced forward. "Think we could invite them here?"

Cullen chuckled as they shared a smile. She was jesting, which was a good sign. The closer they walked to the gate, the tighter her hand clenched his. He heard her ragged breaths, her chest rising and falling quickly.

No words passed between them as they closed the distance to the gate. Cullen's attention was diverted between Tamlyn and the soldiers who stared down at them. He counted five that he could see on the battlements, but there would be many more hidden. These men wore the same armor as those in the forest.

The helm was square with two holes, leaving the eyes minimally exposed. Two wide, wing-like ornaments were attached to the forehead area. The shoulders were rounded and large in size, the armor elongated. There were long, ornamental metal pieces on some as decoration. Cullen realized that it must be their ranking system. The more ornaments, the higher the rank.

Vambraces with many rows of small metal pieces that mimicked dragon scales protected the soldiers' lower arms. Cullen's gaze lowered to the breastplate made of two layers of metal that also mimicked dragon scales. It covered the soldiers from neck to groin. Cullen couldn't see their upper legs, but the soldiers in the forest had had their upper legs covered by rounded half-cuisses. The lower legs by greaves.

These were men well acquainted with battle. An army didn't create armor like that without reason. One wrong move and he and Tamlyn would be barred from entering.

"Trust me," he urged.

A tremor went through her arm to her hand in his. "I don't know why, but I do."

He halted them and looked up at the soldiers. The men stared down at him, talking amongst themselves. His enhanced hearing allowed him to discern that they were betting on whether he and Tamlyn lived in the city or were only visiting.

"What business do you have here?" one of the soldiers demanded of Cullen.

He put a friendly smile on his face and copied their accent. "We're visiting."

Two of the soldiers laughed, and money exchanged hands as the soldier who'd spoken to him motioned to someone Cullen couldn't see. A few moments later, the gates groaned loudly as they cracked open enough for him and Tamlyn to sidle in sideways. Other soldiers waited for them once they were inside the city. Cullen didn't stop. He kept walking.

"I can't believe it worked," Tamlyn whispered, moving close to him as they passed a group of people.

He smiled at her as he pulled her to the wall to get out of the crowd. Cullen glanced toward the gate. "They see what they want to see. They believe that no one with magic would dare enter, and if one did, the soldiers believe they could stop them."

"Look at all the faces," Tamlyn said. Her gaze moved over those passing before them. "They have no idea what is really happening in the city, do they?"

"They might."

Her head swiveled to him. "Then why don't they do something?"

"Folks who have no training in battle going up against an army?" He gave her a flat look. "That is certain death. You said yourself that other villages are no more. I'm guessing most of them came here, believing they would have a better life. No doubt they learned soon enough just what kind of life it is."

She inched closer to him. "Then why don't they leave?"

"Where would they go? They've probably been told there is nowhere else for them to live. They can either lament their life, or they can make do with what they have."

"Like me, Sian, and Jenefer."

"Aye," he said and met her hazel gaze. The sunlight brought out more flecks of gold and bronze in her irises.

Tamlyn drew in a deep breath. As she released it, her shoulders relaxed. "We're in. Now what?"

"I want you to take me around the city. How many levels can we go up?"

She leaned her head back and pointed to the very top. "The four highest levels are for the wealthy. The temple is one below that. The fourth level is where the temple and priests reside."

"What about the army?"

"Every level has a squad that consists of seven to fourteen soldiers."

Cullen considered that information. "And the rest of the army?"

"There's a lower level with the armory. There are also two sets of stables on this level for the soldiers—one on each end. The upper four levels have their own stables."

"Is there just one way up to each level?"

She shook her head. "There is the main road we're on now that switchbacks up each level. There are also stairs that can be used."

"I take it we can rent rooms somewhere."

Tamlyn scratched her ear and turned her head away when two soldiers passed and looked closely at them. "A few places. I have a couple of coins, but the place won't be nice."

"Show me the coins."

She carefully opened a pouch and let him look inside.

Cullen put his hand under the bag to feel the weight. Then he put his hand inside and felt the rough edges of the round coin. He got a good look at either side before using his magic to add twice as many coins, making sure he had some for himself, too.

"What if someone sees?" she hissed.

He released the pouch and stepped back with a smile. "You risk life and limb climbing a wall, but I do *that*, and you make a fuss?"

Her mouth opened, but she decided against whatever she was going to say. Instead, she pulled the strings of the bag closed.

"Shall we?" he asked as he held out his hand.

He was surprised at the happiness he felt at her hand in his. Cullen had offered it thinking it would ease her trepidation, but in the end, he was the one moved by it. Ever since their kiss, he'd been unable to think of anything but her taste and the feel of her. He ached to have her. The fact that they were alone now should make that easier.

There was something between them. It was a fact he couldn't deny. This was the point where he would usually disappear, but that wasn't possible with Tamlyn. He'd given his word, and he intended to keep it. Not to mention, he had his own mission.

He did have a choice, though. He could ignore whatever pulled them together for the sake of his assignment. Or he could give in to it. He didn't want to hurt Tamlyn. He didn't like to hurt anyone, but her most especially. There was something special about her. At first, he'd thought it was because she was a Banshee. Now, he realized it was just her.

Her beauty. Her spirit. Her courage. Her bravery. Her loyalty. The more he learned about her, the more he liked her.

And the more he knew he needed to get away.

She could have lost her life last night. Had he and Jenefer not been there to stop Tamlyn, she would likely be in enemy hands. She and her friends were doing something admirable, worthy. To walk away from them now would be akin to letting them die. That wasn't something he would do.

So, he remained. All the while, putting himself through all kinds of self-inflicted torture for a Banshee he couldn't stop thinking about. One he was now alone with.

He clenched his teeth as his balls tightened when he thought of how her arms had tightened around him during their kiss. How she had held nothing back.

How she had melted against him, seeking the pleasure that awaited them.

Yeah. He was in absolute agony.

"Fuck me," he murmured as he felt his cock hardening.

Tamlyn looked at him. "What's that?"

He shook his head. "Nothing." He only wished it was. The knot growing in his gut told him it was anything but.

Cullen forced himself to focus on the city. The iron oxide in the sandstone gave the stone its reddish hue. It wasn't a natural red, but more of a mixture of pink, brown, beige, and red. The architecture itself was beautiful. It reminded him of the ruins from ancient cities long lost on Earth. Cullen hadn't expected to see such detail in the archways or the columns at the bottom level, but the designers made sure that the beauty of the buildings was from the entrance all the way to the top.

He shifted his attention from the structures to the people. They weren't overtly friendly, but they weren't rude, either. Few paid attention to either him or Tamlyn. The odd ones who did returned a nod or a smile, but that was it.

"I thought everyone would stare at me," Tamlyn said.

He let his gaze linger on her profile, sweeping over her high cheekbones and down her long neck. "You're beautiful enough."

Her head ducked, a smile pulling her lips. Her eyes briefly met his. "That isn't what I meant."

"I know, but I speak the truth. You think you have a target on your back, and in a way, you do. However, these people doona know that. They doona know or care who you are, as long as you doona disrupt their lives."

A smile filled her face when she turned her head to him. "You were right. About everything."

"You know you shouldna say such things to men."

She laughed, the sound musical and soothing. "I won't say that too often, so you needn't worry."

His smile remained long after she looked away. The knot in his stomach grew. He didn't want to enjoy spending time with her like this. It was too…intimate. Like they were lovers and going about their daily lives. His life had no room for a woman. Not even one as spectacular as Tamlyn.

They were on the second level when she pointed to a building on the left. "There's a tavern that has rooms."

"It's a good place to get details of the city. Though that one looks a bit rough."

"It is," she said and jerked her chin farther up the street. "The place on the right is another."

Cullen waited until they reached it to make his decision. It looked better than the first. If he were traveling alone, he might have taken his chances there, but he wasn't alone. He had Tamlyn, and he had to consider several variables. "Any more on this level?"

"One. It's this way."

It wasn't much better than the first or the second. Cullen raised his brows. "Next level?"

Tamlyn walked him to a set of steep stairs that they climbed to the next level. Immediately to his left was another tavern with rooms.

"Of course, you'd choose the most expensive," she laughed when he pulled her toward the door.

Cullen waggled his brows at her. His smile was gone by the time they entered. The place was clean and filled with people. "There's a table in the back. Wait for me there."

She eyed him but didn't argue. He waited until she was seated before walking to the bar. It didn't take long for the balding bartender with a wide girth to make his way over.

"What can I get for you?" the man asked.

Cullen leaned an elbow on the bar and changed his accent to match Tamlyn's. "A room, if you have it."

"Only one left," the man said. "Just you?"

Cullen glanced to the back where Tamlyn sat. "Me and my wife." The instant the words were out, they sounded right.

The man smiled and held out his hand. "I'm Tully. I own the tavern."

Cullen shook with him. "Nice to meet you. I'm Cullen."

"We have excellent food. My daughter has a gift. My wife makes all the desserts, which go fast."

"Thanks for the notice. I'm sure we'll partake."

Cullen joined Tamlyn at the table with two tankards of ale. He set one in front of her before lowering himself into the seat.

"How did you pay? I have the coins," she said and jiggled the pouch at her waist.

He flashed her a smile and kept his voice low so no one would hear his brogue. "Think how you got those."

"You're impossible," she said with a laugh.

He lifted his tankard to her. "But fun."

She shook her head before taking a small drink.

"We have a room," Cullen told her.

Tamlyn looked around the tavern. "Do you want to stay here?"

"For a bit. I'm sure we can pick up some things if we listen hard enough. But later, I'd like to see more of the city. We'll finish our drinks before we go to our room."

"Our?" she replied softly.

He met her gaze. "There's no way I'm allowing you to stay in a room by yourself here. Besides, there was only one left."

"I didn't want that anyway," she retorted and shot him a sly look.

Cullen shifted in his chair. He could hardly wait until tonight. If she kept looking at him like that, he'd take her upstairs right now.

Chapter Seventeen

Now wasn't the time for Tamlyn's thoughts to be on ripping Cullen's clothes off, but that's exactly where they were. Holding his hand all morning, seeing those sexy smiles, and being so near to him were doing crazy things to her. She should be a bundle of nerves now that she was in Stonemore, and yet all she could think about was when she could kiss Cullen again.

"Lass," he warned in a low voice, his eyes darkening with desire.

"Shouldn't we check the room?" Her voice sounded breathless and needy. She had never heard herself sound like that before. Then again, she had never encountered a Dragon King before.

Without a word, he stood and held out his hand. She took it, her heart racing. Chills raced up her arm when his fingers closed over hers. He didn't take his eyes from hers when he led her around the table and through the room to the stairs.

Someone called out Cullen's name. He glanced over and caught the keys to the room in midair without breaking stride. Her heart thudded against her ribs as her blood heated in her veins. Then they were in a room. Tamlyn grabbed his head and brought it down to hers, pressing her lips against his.

The kiss was all that she remembered and more. He teased and tempted, then demanded and devoured. She was breathless with need. No one had ever made her feel this way. And she knew there was no one else on this realm, or another, who ever could.

His arms wrapped around her tightly. She loved the feel of him pressed against her, all his hard muscles. He splayed his hand and slowly moved it down her back to cup her butt as he ground against her. She moaned when she felt his rigid arousal. Tamlyn wound her arms about his neck and rocked her hips against his.

He tore his mouth from hers and said in a husky voice, "God, I want you."

Tamlyn pushed him away and stepped back. She held his gaze as she removed her belt then pulled her shirt over her head and let it drop. A groan ripped from him as he yanked his shirt off so hard it tore. Then he reached for her, hauling her against his hard body once more. His lips took hers in a scorching kiss that left her shaking and breathless for more.

He backed her across the room then lifted her and gently laid her on the bed. Next thing she knew, their clothes were gone, and they were flesh to flesh. She rolled him onto his back and ended the kiss so she could look at him.

She ran her fingers lightly over his wide chest and chiseled abs down to his trim hips. Her gaze landed on his cock, hard and throbbing. She wrapped her fingers around his shaft. Tamlyn glanced at him to see his gaze locked on her hand. She moved her hand up and down his length, learning the feel of him.

* * * *

Cullen forced himself to lay still and allow Tamlyn her time to touch him. She left a trail of fire from his chest down to his rod. When she took him in hand, he fought not to rock his hips up. Then she began to move her hand. It was the most exquisite pleasure he had ever experienced.

A jolt ran through him when she circled her thumb over the sensitive head of his arousal. He hissed at the sensations that shot through him like lightning. He couldn't lay still anymore. It was his turn to play.

He flipped her onto her back. A surprise cry fell from her lips as she blinked up at him. Then that stunning mouth of hers curved into a knowing smile.

"My turn," he said.

His gaze moved down her face to her chest. Her breasts were large enough to fill his hands, her dark-tipped nipples hard and waiting for his mouth. He ran a finger down the valley between her breasts and watched as she held her breath. Her lashes lowered briefly. He caressed down her stomach pausing to circle her navel twice before continuing down to the triangle of black curls between her legs.

The minute he cupped her sex, she moaned loudly and covered his hand with hers. He moved his gaze to her face as he began to leisurely stroke her. Her lips parted as she sighed in pleasure. He pushed a finger inside her, feeling her wet heat. Her hand moved up his arm to his shoulder as her lashes batted open. He found himself looking into her hazel eyes, lost in the pleasure and need that consumed them both.

She pulled his head down to hers and kissed him as gently as he fondled her. Her hips rocked softly against his hand. It wasn't until he found her clit that her body quivered. Her legs fell open, inviting him to do more. Cullen didn't need to be told twice.

He kissed down her jaw and neck, along her collarbones and over the swells of her breasts until his lips closed over a turgid peak. Her back arched, a startled cry falling from her swollen lips. He suckled a nipple as he teased her clit mercilessly. The louder her cries became, the more he needed to hear them.

Cullen moved to her other nipple. Her nails dug into his back before her body stiffened for a heartbeat. He watched the pleasure wash over her face as she orgasmed, her body moving with the spasms. His cock jumped. How he wished he could've felt that. But he would soon. Very soon.

* * * *

Tamlyn was sure she was floating. Her body hummed with the force of the climax. She hadn't experienced anything like that before. It was…she couldn't find the words to describe the beauty or amazing intensity of it.

She sank her fingers into Cullen's thick hair when he began to kiss down her stomach. There was so much she wanted to do to his body, but she needed to recover first. Her limbs felt weighted, her eyes heavy.

They snapped open in shock when his tongue flicked over her sensitive clit. She gasped at the new bliss that rushed through her. Tamlyn didn't have the energy to stop him, and it felt too good anyway. She relaxed and let his tongue lick and lave her. Just as she closed her eyes to give in to the pleasure, he slid a finger inside her. The movement of his finger in and out of her, along with his tongue on her clit had her clutching the covers. Desire coiled low in her belly and grew with each stroke.

She rocked her hips, seeking the release she knew was coming.

Cullen's mouth and finger were suddenly gone. She opened her eyes to see him kneeling between her legs, his gaze on her face. Only then did he guide his cock to her and push inside.

The feel of him stretching her was wonderful. Then he was over her, his body moving, his hips thrusting. She wrapped her legs around his waist and moved with him, allowing him to sink deeper.

* * * *

Cullen had known being inside Tamlyn would be amazing. He hadn't expected this, however. Her body, her touch, her moans. All of it sent him spiraling into an abyss of need that he would never claw his way out of.

And he wasn't sure he wanted to.

It was as if they were synced on a level that seemed impossible to comprehend. Yet it was there for him to feel, even if he couldn't see it. The proof was before him. Even as his mind cautioned him, his body demanded more of the beauty in his arms.

The fire, the passion within her matched his perfectly. He tried to hold back from her, but she wouldn't let him. She demanded he give as much as she. And he was powerless to refuse. He thrust harder, deeper, joining their bodies in a dance as old as time—fusing their essences, their souls as nothing else could.

He stared into her eyes. Everything suddenly made sense. He couldn't explain it, and he didn't want to.

"Cullen," she whispered as she bit her lip.

The first clench of her sex around him, and he was overcome with his orgasm. It slammed into him, barreling through. He gasped at the power of it, shocked to find they had reached fulfillment together.

He slowly pulled out of her and rolled to his side. She turned her head to him and smiled before turning onto her side. He'd always run when things got too familiar. The emotions within him had exceeded familiar, but he didn't want to leave. He wanted to stay. With Tamlyn. It sounded odd, even to him, but that was the truth. They reached for each other at the same time. He couldn't stop kissing her.

Cullen smoothed a curl off her cheek and smiled. "Och, lass. I think you've ruined me for anyone else."

"Don't tease," she said.

He rolled onto his back and waited until she laid her head on his chest before wrapping his arm around her. "I'm no'."

She was silent for a long moment. "I know you've ruined me for anyone else."

Her words rang in his ears. Giving in to his need for her had put him somewhere he had never wanted to be—close to a woman. He'd known he was going down a road he'd never traveled before, but damn if he could make himself deviate. Even now, he was content. Happy, even.

Cullen cleared his throat, forcing his mind off such thoughts. "What now?"

"Can't we just enjoy this moment a bit longer?"

He kissed her forehead. "That's an excellent idea. I wish I would've thought of it myself."

"I usually have great ideas."

He chuckled and closed his eyes. Their legs remained intertwined as she draped over his chest. This was the exact position he'd never wanted to find himself in. He had run from anything even resembling it. Now, he was ready to fight anyone and anything that dared to destroy…whatever this was.

He didn't want to name it. And he didn't think she did either. There was no reason to. Things might look different in the light of day. It was a good thing no one asked him what this was then, because he might very well have said love.

Chapter Eighteen

Lips on her neck pulled Tamlyn from sleep. A hard body was pressed against her back. She sighed as the soft lips moved over a sensitive spot.

"About time you woke."

She smiled at Cullen's teasing tone. Her eyes opened to see the sunlight coming through the windows. She hadn't realized that she had fallen asleep. But, oh, how good it felt to be in his arms.

His hand cupped her breast, gently massaging it. "I thought you might be hungry."

Tamlyn's breath caught when his breath fanned over her ear right before he gently nipped her lobe with his teeth. She turned in his arms and shoved him onto his back so she could straddle his hips. The feel of his hard cock against her sex made her nipples harden in expectation.

"I'm hungry, all right," she said in a soft voice as she seductively leaned over him then gave him a soft kiss.

His hands came to her hips. "I should warn you that it isna a good idea to tease a Dragon King."

"Who said I'm teasing?" she asked with a smile.

His pale brown eyes intensified as he lifted her with his hands. She balanced on her knees while taking his arousal and bringing it to her center. The blunt head of his staff rubbed against her before sliding inside. She released a sigh of contentment as she lowered herself onto him. His hands returned to her hips. She placed her palms on his chest and began to rock her hips back and forth.

He sat up and claimed her mouth in a scorching kiss while their bodies moved against each other. The friction between them left her breathless, while his kiss stole her senses. She didn't know what it was about Cullen that fascinated and charmed her. All she knew was that she wanted to be with him.

In every way possible.

Tamlyn suddenly found herself on her hands and knees. A large hand splayed on her back. She looked over her shoulder to see Cullen kneeling behind her as he guided himself to her entrance. With one thrust, he buried himself inside her again.

She moaned at the sensation of him filling her so perfectly, so…completely. Her fingers dug into the covers as he held her hips and rocked his, driving into her repeatedly as he increased his tempo. She was lost in a dream-like state with her body flooded with desire, and Cullen pushing her to her limits.

Somehow, it was everything she needed. She hadn't even known it. How could he?

Then he was leaning over her, one large hand on her lower neck as he gently turned her head. His lips brushed against hers as he thrust hard and deep.

"Come with me," he whispered in a sexy voice.

As if he had some power over her body, she gasped when she found herself on the edge of climax. He continued his rhythm, sinking harder, deeper inside her.

"Aye," he murmured, his breath fanning her cheek. "Let me feel you."

Tamlyn cried out as pleasure flooded her body. She barely felt his fingers dig into her hips or heard his shout of completion, she was so emersed in her own ecstasy. Her arms gave out and she fell on her stomach.

Cullen slowly lowered himself over her, gathered her in his arms, and rolled onto his side. He kissed her cheek as they lay together in silence. She kept her eyes closed, hovering somewhere between sleep and wakefulness. He never stopped touching her, caressing her, almost as if he didn't want her to forget that he was there. As if she could.

"Is it always like that?" she asked. "I've had few experiences."

"Nay, lass. It isna always like that."

Something in his voice made her frown. Just as she was about to ask, her stomach growled loudly.

Cullen laughed as he sat up. "I think it's time for food."

"Do we have to go down now?" she asked as she looked at him.

"We doona have to leave this room. What would you like to eat? I'll have it here in a blink."

Tamlyn sat up as a thought took root. "How about your favorite dish from your realm?"

"If you want."

She considered that for a moment. "Do you even need to eat?"

"No' really."

"What about sleep?"

He shrugged nonchalantly. "No' if we doona want to."

"How old are you exactly?"

Brown eyes slid to her. "Think of a huge number. The biggest number you can imagine. Now triple it. That still willna come close to my age."

"How do you do it? How do you go on?"

Cullen walked naked to the window, giving her a view of his amazing backside. He stared out the glass for a long moment. "This conversation is better with some food."

No sooner had he said the words than a round, wooden table and chairs appeared. On it were two plates and several dishes of food. She rose from the bed and went to look. Some of the dishes looked similar to things she had eaten on Zora, but she wasn't taking anything for granted.

She glanced at Cullen, but he kept his gaze outside. Tamlyn grabbed the blanket from the bed, wound it around herself, and sat. The longer he remained quiet, the more she regretted her question. He'd been so open about everything, that she hadn't considered there could be things he wouldn't wish to speak about.

He turned to her with a smile that didn't quite reach his eyes. He strode to the table and looked at the dishes. "These are foods from various regions on my realm. I thought you could get a taste of some of my favorites."

"Thank you," she said with a big smile. Her stomach rumbled again, reminding her that she was hungry.

Cullen pointed to the first dish. "Insalata Caprese. It's made with buffalo mozzarella—a cheese—then a tomato, and topped with a fresh sprig of basil and seasoned with salt and olive oil. It's a simple Italian salad."

Tamlyn's mouth was watering before he finished. She found a fork and knife to cut a slice. The instant she took a bite, there was an explosion of flavor in her mouth. She wanted to devour the entire plate, but there was so much more on the table.

"That was delicious."

Cullen grinned. "I'm glad."

She pointed to another plate and the interesting things on it. "What about this?"

"Ah. A classic dish from France. Cognac shrimp with *beurre blanc*, which simply means a butter and wine sauce."

Tamlyn speared a shrimp with her fork and took a small bite. The flavors together were amazing. Once she swallowed, she ate the rest of the shrimp and looked at him to choose the next dish.

Cullen looked over the table and pointed to one. "Haggis is a staple in Scotland."

"What's in it?"

He opened his mouth, then closed it. "Perhaps it's better if I doona tell you."

Tamlyn shrugged and cut into it. The minute she put it in her mouth, she wanted to spit it out. Somehow, she managed to swallow it. "I think I'll pass on that."

"I figured," Cullen said with a laugh. "Try the smoked salmon. It's a fish."

She shrugged and took a bite, nodding with pleasure. "I like this."

"It's also from Scotland."

"What's that?" she asked and pointed to the large, round piece of food.

"That is an American cuisine, though it originated in Italy. The Americans made it their own. It's called pizza. It's—"

It smelled so good she didn't wait for him to finish, just picked up a slice to put on her plate. She thought about cutting it but ended up bringing the small end to her mouth and taking a bite. "Oh. This is good," she said around a mouthful.

Cullen shook his head and sank into the empty chair. "I'm surprised you waited until last."

She laughed and put more into her mouth. She studied him as she chewed. After she swallowed, she asked, "How did you become King of your clan?"

Cullen paused for a moment. "With difficulty."

"That isn't an answer."

"It's the truth," he replied. "The Garnets had been at war with the Black clan. Neither clan could get an advantage for verra long. It was a war that should no' have ever happened. Our King let the power of his position go to his head. I felt the call from the magic before we began the war, but I was young and unsure of what I felt. Once he instigated the war, and I saw so many of my clan die, I challenged him. I was still young. My older brothers thought I'd lost my mind. My parents were so shocked, they couldna react. My little sister offered to hide me."

She watched as a smile pulled at his lips when he spoke of his family. It'd never entered her mind that he'd had family, though it should have. She was embarrassed at her thoughtlessness. Tamlyn took another bite of pizza, enthralled with his tale.

Cullen's brown eyes met hers. He picked a piece of meat from the pizza and popped it into his mouth, licking his fingers. "Our King had been challenged before. I watched each one. All dragons did. It allowed me to study him and his moves. His downfall was underestimating me." Cullen took a deep breath and released it. "Our battle was brutal. His first strike knocked me flat. Everything hurt so badly, I didna want to get up. But I had to. We fought for hours. The longer I remained, the more I saw the fear in his eyes. The only way a King takes the position from another is with death. I didna want to end his life, but it's what the magic demanded."

He looked away, his eyes going distant. "I delivered the killing blow. He fell hard, but he wasna dead. He motioned me close as he lay dying and told me he didna understand why the magic had taken the position from him. The light went out of his eyes before I could answer. I'm no' sure what I would've said anyway." Cullen sucked in a breath and lifted his gaze to her. "I immediately contacted the King of Blacks, and our conflict ended that day."

She swallowed the last of the pizza and smiled at him. "I'm sorry you had to go through that, but it appears the magic was right in choosing you."

"Maybe."

Tamlyn had been eyeing the mark on his arm. She jerked her chin to it. "What is that?"

Cullen glanced at his biceps. "A tattoo. Do you no' have them there?"

"I've never seen one, but I've not gone many places. Why do you have it?"

"Every Dragon King has one. Tattoos on my realm are popular. Some humans are covered with them. But none have the mix of red and black ink that marks us. All of us have a dragon on different parts of our body."

She let her gaze roam over the dragon that covered his entire arm from head to tail. It appeared as if the dragon were crawling up Cullen's arm. The head of the animal rested on his shoulder, while its wings were slightly spread, and its tail dangled to his wrist.

"I like it," she told him.

He winked at her. "I think it's a good thing my shirt is long-sleeved to cover it."

They shared a laugh. Tamlyn's gaze returned to the table. The only thing she hadn't tasted sat in the middle. She raised her brows, waiting.

"It's a dessert from Mexico," Cullen explained. "It's called *tres leches* cake."

"I need to taste that."

He took pity on her and cut her a slice to put on her plate.

The bite was divine. She couldn't even spare a word before she had to have another taste. When she looked up, she saw Cullen watching her with a peculiar expression she couldn't quite name. They had an easy silence, despite the tension she'd felt earlier after asking how he'd lived so long. She wasn't going to bring that up again. If he didn't want to talk about it, she wouldn't press him.

Tamlyn sat back now that her stomach was full. "Thank you for this. I want to eat more of it later."

"You wanted to know how I've lived so long."

Her smile slipped. "You don't have to tell me."

"The truth is, I've no' thought about it. We do what we have to do, and the Dragon Kings have to survive. We must protect our realm. Now that we've located the dragons, we doona have to worry about that anymore. Yet, that opens up other concerns. We're powerful, and beings like us tend to have a lot of enemies."

She glanced at the floor. "I can imagine."

"You can no'," he said, though there was no anger in his words. "We lost our purpose when the dragons left our realm. We believed at first that they would return, but as the centuries turned into millennia, we realized we clung to a false hope. Our focus shifted to protecting ourselves and Dreagan at all costs. There are times I couldna handle our life, and I'd find my mountain and sleep."

"Sleep?" she asked with a frown.

"I've slept for thousands of years. It's easier than walking among the mortals sometimes. If a dragon goes too deep in the dragon sleep, they can slip into that dream world and never return."

Tamlyn drew her legs up against her chest beneath the blanket. "Is that what you wanted?"

"A few times I wouldna have minded it. Being this age isna an easy burden. I've seen so verra much. Sometimes, it doesna affect me because I know things will change eventually. Other times, I can no' sit by and do nothing. Yet, nothing changes for me."

"You really can't die?"

"Only by another Dragon King."

Her eyes widened. "Do you all fight often?"

"We're brothers. We bicker, aye, but we doona battle to the death."

That was something, at least.

"I doona know how long I'll walk this realm or another. I could live for dozens more millennia, or I could die tomorrow. I was given this role as a Dragon King for a reason, and I never let myself forget it."

Chapter Nineteen

The last thing Cullen wanted to do was leave the room. There were those who wanted to capture Tamlyn. Which meant they would likely set another trap for her by murdering another child. He needed to be prepared for anything, and unfortunately, that meant seeing more of the city.

After such heavy talk and filling their stomachs, he and Tamlyn walked from the tavern onto the crowded street. He immediately wanted to return to their room. They could be themselves there. He didn't have to hide his accent, and she didn't have to worry about being discovered. Cullen couldn't remember the last time he had wanted to retreat from anything.

It had nothing to do with fear and everything to do with protecting Tamlyn, her friends, and his friends and family.

He did a double-take, his gaze narrowed as he looked through the crowd. He saw something out of the corner of his eye. This was the second time he'd caught a glimpse of it, and the second time he'd let it out of his sight.

"What is it?" Tamlyn asked.

He turned his head to her. "Nothing."

"I can handle the truth. It's lies that mess things up."

Cullen sighed at being called out. "I saw something."

"What?"

"I'm no' sure. It was out of the corner of my eye. A flicker or something." He fisted his hands in frustration. "I saw it right when we entered the city, but I didna pay it much heed. This time, I did. It's there, but when I look at it, it's gone."

Tamlyn took one of his fists between her hands and moved closer. "A person?"

"That's just it. I can no' tell."

"Things can't just disappear."

But they could. He didn't want to frighten her. Besides, if this were the enemy he searched for, it was only after dragons. Tamlyn and those in Stonemore should be safe. Yet...why hadn't it come after him?

Unease settled awkwardly in his belly.

"Tell me," Tamlyn demanded.

He glanced around. "Show me the rest of the city. I need to see important places, areas we could hide, spots that others might lie in wait, and form exit strategies."

"I'll try."

Cullen linked his fingers with hers, and they set out. There was a concert of sounds with the voices, animals, and the clink of the soldiers' armor. They walked along the third level while Tamlyn pointed out different places. Cullen paused to take a closer look at a few. The buildings were such that there was no room wasted for alleys. Though there *were* two places that would be good hiding spots for them. He pointed them out to Tamlyn.

He took special interest on the fourth level where the temple was located. They took their time walking past the priests' living quarters. Tamlyn shook so violently, he worried she wouldn't make it, but he should've known better. She was strong. She'd proven it by continuing on when she could've turned back.

"We won't be able to get to the other levels," she warned when they stopped in front of the temple.

Cullen walked to the alcove before the temple that showed the impressive view of the city and the forest below. They were higher than the treetops. He could see the canyon from this vantage point, but humans would have a difficult time.

"Show me how you get the children," he whispered.

She turned him to face the temple and plastered on a fake smile while nodding to the left side of the building. "There's a narrow walkway for the priests to get to the back of the temple. I use that to get to the wall."

His gaze moved up the nearly flat stonework. It was only because he looked for the places for climbing that he found them. There were three windows near the top.

"Which window?" he asked.

She turned her back to the temple. "Middle."

Of course, it would be the highest one. She must have climbed nearly three stories to reach it. Not only had she scaled up the structure, but she'd descended with kids in her arms or on her back. Cullen could hardly believe it. He was both impressed by her courage and angered at her lack of concern for her safety.

"Don't say it," she warned.

He glanced at her before turning his attention back to the temple. His gaze moved over faces, looking for anyone or anything that stood out. "What?"

"That you think I'm crazy for doing this. I can't help it. I have to."

"Aye, lass, I know. I witnessed it last night."

She sighed. "Thank you."

His attention was caught when the crowd began to part and quiet. That's when he caught sight of some men in red robes. "What do the priests wear?"

Tamlyn stiffened beside him. He reached down and took her clammy hand in his. She squeezed his fingers.

"They willna harm you," he promised her. "I willna let them."

That vow seemed to allow her to take a deep breath. It took her three tries before she was able to articulate her thoughts. "They wear red robes. The more trimmings on them, the higher their rank."

"What about the ones in armor?"

"Chosen by the Divine to become priests. Until then, they will protect the priests and temple above all else."

Cullen watched as the progression of priests and soldiers filed into the temple. A few moments later, the door shut with a loud boom. The crowd found their voices again and went about their day.

He squeezed Tamlyn's hand to let her know that he was there. Suddenly, the hairs on the back of his neck stood on end. Someone was watching him. He looked over the temple, but he couldn't see anyone in the windows or elsewhere. That's when he realized it was someone behind him. He turned and let his gaze slowly move over those below him and the buildings, but he still couldn't find anyone.

"How do you get out?" Cullen whispered.

Tamlyn hurried away, tugging him with her. She didn't say anything until they were on the main level, and she'd paused beside a drainage ditch. They exchanged a look.

He smiled at her. "Brave, lass."

"Or crazy," she said with a grin.

Cullen glanced around them to see if anyone was listening. He moved closer to Tamlyn, pressing her against the wall and lowering his voice. "We need to come up with a plan. I need to know that you can get out of here if you have to."

"They'll be waiting for me in the forest even if I do. Besides, I'm not leaving without you."

"It's a precaution. It's better to be safe and think of all options beforehand."

She nodded in understanding. "We should probably return to the tavern to do that."

They made their way back to the third level and the tavern and took the same table in the back that they'd used that morning. The pub was filling up fast as the sun began its descent. Cullen kept his back to a corner so he could see the door and the stairs leading up to the rooms. Most tables were full, with people laughing and talking. Only one or two individuals sat alone, content to lose themselves in their alcohol.

"Is there someplace you can go other than the woods?" he asked in a low voice.

Tamlyn shrugged and shot him a dark look. "We shouldn't talk about this here."

"We aren't. It was just a question."

"What's going on? Something changed."

He would have to tell her eventually. Might as well be now. "Nothing specific. Just a gut feeling."

"As long as you've been around? I trust your gut."

Cullen's lips softened into a smile. "I hope I'm wrong."

"Like you said, it's better to be safe than sorry."

He wanted to be wrong. He wished he was, but he wasn't. Between the things he'd seen out of the corner of his eye and the feeling of being watched, he knew he wasn't. He leaned over the table and took her hand in his. "If you can no' get back to Jenefer and Sian, you need to get to my friends."

"Are you insane?" she asked in a choked whisper.

"They know about you. Tell them who you are. Tell them what we were about."

She shook her head of black curls. "You can do that. You can get away."

"I can and I will. This is in case you can no'. Remember my vow?"

"Yes," she said with a heavy sigh.

He raised his brows and nodded. "That's what I'm thinking about. If you can no' get to your friends, go to mine. They will protect you until I can get to you."

"I don't like the idea of going without you."

Cullen's heart clenched at her words. "Me, either."

"Then let's not. We can leave now. We don't have to stay."

But they did—and she knew it.

He rubbed his thumb across the back of her hand. "Remember who you are."

"I do."

He left it at that. Now wasn't the time to explain it to her. Cullen sat back in his chair, but he didn't release her hand. He'd felt a deep connection to Tamlyn since the first time he saw her. Now, that link was stronger. It was, in fact, unbreakable.

The thing Cullen had run from his entire life sat across from him now. His mate. He'd suspected from the beginning, but he hadn't wanted to contemplate it, much less admit it. Now that he had, he didn't know where that left him. They were in a viper's nest. He'd vowed to protect her. Cullen hoped he could do that and keep his promise to his friends, too.

They remained in the tavern for another hour. He listened to many conversations, but he heard nothing that could give them an advantage. Finally, he'd had enough. He needed to be alone with her. He caught Tamlyn's gaze and glanced at the stairs. She nodded, and they rose together. On the way up, he saw a few people who looked their way. Though none would meet his gaze when he looked at them.

In their chamber with the door locked, he pulled Tamlyn into his arms and simply held her. She said nothing as she wrapped her arms around him. The darker the night became, the more apprehensive he was. That meant it was time to talk to Con.

"I need to speak to my friends," he told her.

Tamlyn leaned back to look at him. "Should I leave?"

"Stay. I willna be long."

He waited until she was on the bed before he walked to the window and opened the link. *"Con. Brandr. Eurwen. Vaughn."*

One by one, they answered him, creating an open link between all five of them.

"*I was getting concerned,*" Con said.

Cullen braced his hands on either side of the window. "*I'm in Stonemore. Things have progressed rapidly.*"

"*Tell us,*" Eurwen urged.

Cullen filled everyone in on things from the moment he left dragon land until that day, though he left out certain details about his time with Tamlyn.

"*Bloody hell,*" Vaughn murmured.

Brandr said, "*If you think our adversary is there, then we need to come to you.*"

"*No,*" Cullen said. "*The army was waiting for Tamlyn last night. They'll set another trap for her. That's why we're in the city. I willna leave her alone.*"

Con made an indistinct sound. "*You doona know what to expect from these priests or the soldiers.*"

"*They sacrifice children. That tells me everything,*" Eurwen snapped.

Cullen agreed with her. "*Eurwen, you said the thing that attacked you was invisible. I've seen things out of the corner of my eye, but when I look, nothing is there.*"

"*That's exactly what I saw,*" she said.

Brandr huffed in outrage. "*So many things could go sideways while you and Tamlyn are there.*"

"*He's a Dragon King,*" Con replied.

That was his way of reminding Cullen of his duties and his vow. They came first before anyone or anything else.

"*Con, you might be asking a lot of him,*" Vaughn said.

Cullen took a deep breath. "*I have it under control. If there's a hiccup, I'm sending Tamlyn to our side. Just take care of her and help get her to the canyon until I can get there.*"

"*We will,*" Eurwen promised.

Chapter Twenty

Tamlyn's stomach churned with uneasiness. Cullen was rattled, and that worried her. Her gaze didn't leave him as he stood with his back to her. She couldn't imagine communicating with anyone via her mind, but she'd like to try it. It would certainly make things easier. There was a lot she would like to tell Sian and Jenefer on the off chance she didn't make it back to the ruins.

The day had been filled with the highest of highs, and she suspected the lowest of the lows was coming. She wanted to say it was just her imagination, but she knew it wasn't. Something had been watching Cullen. She hadn't seen anything, but he had significantly more magic than she did. And she trusted him.

She'd put up a fuss about him when they first met, but now couldn't remember why. Jenefer's aversion to Cullen made it easy for Tamlyn to keep him at arm's length. How silly she had been. Though, no doubt Jenefer would tell her she was being idiotic now. Just because Cullen was a Dragon King didn't automatically make him an ally.

Jenefer was right. But Cullen had proven time and again that he could be trusted. Tamlyn, Jenefer, and Sian had become so accustomed to relying solely on their trio that they had forgotten what it was like to trust and welcome a helping hand. They'd had to be vigilant and careful for so long, they had forgotten how to recognize a possible friend.

Tamlyn wanted to go to Cullen and wrap her arms around him. Instead, she remained on the bed, waiting until he finished. When he finally did turn around, his smile was tight.

"Did you speak to them?" she asked.

He nodded and walked to the bed. "I've filled them in on everything."

"Everything?" she asked with a raise of her brows.

Cullen chuckled. "No' everything."

"What now?"

"Can you draw the upper levels?"

She wrinkled her nose as she scooted off the bed. "I've never been past the fourth level. I've always assumed it's the same as the bottom four, but I have no knowledge to support that."

"Do you remember the places I showed you that would be hiding spots?"

Tamlyn nodded.

"Good." He walked to the table. Before he reached it, a white, three-dimensional replica of the city appeared.

She hurried to stare in wonder. "This makes the city look so inconsequential."

"Stonemore was designed and built well. Their defenses are impressive. The way the wall encloses the city in the mountains ensures that enemies have to attack from the front only since the range is so steep. The builders wouldn't have trapped everyone within the city. There's at least one other way out."

Tamlyn looked at him. "I've never found it. I was lucky to find the drain. I still can't believe they've not realized that's how I've been getting in and out."

"They'll discover it soon enough."

"Which means I need to find another way in."

His brows snapped together. "Meaning, they'll prevent you from getting in. You'll either be caught or you'll have to forgo helping the children here."

"That isn't an option." She stated the words clearly so he would understand how important it was for her.

Cullen dropped his chin to his chest and sighed before looking at her. "I understand. More than you realize, but if you continue, they *will* capture you. Jenefer and Sian will come for you, and then they'll be seized. Who will help the children then?"

"You just want me to walk away?" she asked in disbelief.

"Stonemore can no' be the only city doing this. There are other kids who need help. Leave this city alone for a wee bit and help others. Eventually, you can return."

She turned and walked away a few steps. Tamlyn whirled around and put her hands on her hips. "I don't know if I can. It's not just about rescuing the kids. It's about stopping the people doing these atrocious acts."

"I understand. I really do." He motioned to the model with his head and began to point out where he'd noticed soldiers. "Did you see others?"

"I didn't see half of *those*," she confessed.

"Do the priests stay mainly in the temple?"

She shrugged and shook her head. "I can't answer for certain."

Cullen crossed his arms over his chest and gave her a flat look. "You came into this city without information and climbed up a sheer wall to rescue kids without knowing what you could be facing?"

"When you say it like that, it sounds reckless."

"Because it is. You've been lucky."

She blew out a breath. "I know."

"Partly because they were no' aware of what was going on. They're starting to smarten up if last night was any indication."

Tamlyn didn't need to be told that her time was running out here. She'd known that, but to hear it said so simply made it more of a reality. Sian and Jenefer didn't know what she did, they hadn't seen it. Cullen had.

The thought of leaving any child behind sickened her. But Cullen was right. Other children needed help. How could she get them out of a horrible situation if she was imprisoned? Or worse, dead. Her shoulders slumped as reality became clear.

"My thought is they'll try to lure you out again tonight," he said. "They'll keep their focus on the forest. That gives us valuable time to get the child free."

"And out of the city, right?" she asked when he didn't finish.

His jaw worked as if he were trying to find the words.

"If we stay, they'll find us. The only way the child has a chance is if we get them out of Stonemore."

Cullen ran his hand down his face. "It'll be tricky to get out, but I can do it."

"*We* can do it," she reminded him.

He smiled at her and took her hand. "I'll be helping with the rescue, as well."

"Honestly, I'll be happy not to have to climb that wall by myself again." She let him pull her against him. Tamlyn placed her other hand on his chest as she gazed into his brown eyes. "You're risking a lot to help me."

He shrugged one shoulder. "We have the advantage right now. This may be the only time we have it."

"What about your watcher?"

"It's probably nothing."

She quirked a brow at him. "Really? You're going to try that?"

Cullen laughed softly and glanced away. "You have enough worries."

"We've built trust. Don't destroy that by trying to protect me. Lying isn't protecting."

"Point taken," he said softly. "I've got a bad feeling all the way around. With whoever had eyes on me, a trap for you, and us getting out of the city."

She swallowed and tamped down the fear that'd begun to claw its way back. "Like you said, we have the advantage."

Bells began to toll loudly. They exchanged a look and rushed to the window but saw nothing. Cullen strode to the door and opened it.

"Hey," Cullen called. "What's going on with the bells?"

"Someone has brought in children with magic," said a disembodied voice.

Tamlyn's stomach dropped to her feet. Had he just said *children*?

"More than one?" Cullen asked.

Tamlyn couldn't make out what the man said next. Cullen then shut the door and faced her.

"What?" she asked. "How many?"

He slowly walked to her without looking away. "Five."

"Five?" She covered her mouth with her hand, dazed by the news. Her arm dropped to her side as she looked helplessly around the room.

Cullen moved to stand before her. He cupped her face with his hands, forcing her to look at him. "Like I said, it's a trap."

"What do we do?"

"Nothing."

She blinked up at him, wondering if he was addled. "I have to do something."

"We do nothing right now," he told her in a soothing voice. "There's nothing we *can* do."

"We can plan."

He ran his palms down her arms and took her hands in his. "We'll most likely have a long night. You willna help yourself or the children if you allow worry to consume you."

"Too late," she snapped pithily.

Cullen grinned despite her tone. "Your mind needs to be clear and focused."

"I don't know how to do that. All I know to do is what I've been doing."

"How did you first figure out how to get into the city?"

She started to answer but hesitated. "I'm not sure."

"Is that how the woman who rescued you got you out?"

The harder she tried to remember, the further the memory receded. "I-I'm not sure. Maybe. I don't remember much of that night."

"You were young, aye?"

"And scared."

He pulled her close and wrapped his arms around her. "You knew how to get into the city somehow. My guess is the Banshee who freed you."

It made sense, but for some reason, Tamlyn didn't think that was the answer. She didn't know why, just a feeling within her. She didn't say more to Cullen since she couldn't explain anything.

"I have a few ideas," he said.

Tamlyn leaned back to look at him. "Tell me."

He brought her to the model of the city. Despite his order not to worry, she couldn't help it. Neither of them knew the city or its occupants well. She had been inside the walls, but she had been focused on getting in, reaching the kids, and getting out. She listened as he went through two plans. One where they stayed together, and another where they split up.

She shook her head. "I don't like us splitting up."

"It might be the only option."

That's when it dawned on her. "Because you think someone is here for you?"

"This could be the person who has killed dragons. He nearly killed Eurwen, and he injured Brandr. Had Con not been there, Brandr might verra well have died."

"You want to face this person on your own? I don't think that's smart."

Cullen flashed her a charming smile. "I came to get information on a new enemy. I didna expect to come face-to-face with them, but I'm prepared if I do."

"You didn't think they were those with magic either, did you?"

He briefly looked away. "I should have. We all should've. Maybe the others did and didna tell me. It makes sense. Dragons are no' easy to kill."

"You said Eurwen and Brandr were hurt."

"Aye," he replied with a nod.

"She's a Queen and he's a King. How could they have been hurt? You said only Kings could kill Kings. Is there a Dragon King on our side you don't know about?"

Cullen's brow furrowed in thought. "Fuck me."

Chapter Twenty-one

Cullen sat in the dark with his elbows on his knees and his head in his hands. He'd managed to convince Tamlyn to lay down with him. It wasn't until after she had fallen asleep that he'd risen and walked to the table. His mind hadn't stopped since her statement earlier.

He'd tried to think of other ways someone could take down a Dragon King, but he couldn't find one. It was time he spoke with Constantine.

"Con," he called, opening the link. When there wasn't an immediate response, Cullen tried again.

He didn't think Con would've returned to Earth with Cullen on the human side of the barrier, but he had to admit there might have been something Con had to see to. So, he tried Vaughn.

Again, nothing.

Worry began to set in.

"Brandr. Eurwen," Cullen called.

"Cullen?" Brandr answered.

Relief poured through him as he lifted his head. *"We've overlooked something."*

"Cullen? I can no' hear you. Cullen?"

"Brandr!" he yelled.

But the connection was gone. Cullen tried again and again, but he couldn't get through to anyone. It reminded him of what had happened to Varek when they'd held him as a prisoner in Orgate. Was someone in Stonemore preventing magic from being used?

To test that, Cullen produced a bottle of Dreagan whisky. He looked at it sitting on the table beside him, proof that he could use magic. If someone wasn't preventing him from using his powers, that meant they were preventing him from speaking with the Kings.

The humans on Zora knew very little about dragons and nothing about the Kings. It stood to reason that it had to be someone familiar with the Dragon Kings to understand how they communicated. It would also mean that whoever took it upon themselves to prevent him from reaching out to his friends was extremely powerful.

And in Stonemore.

That's who he'd felt watching him. Cullen hadn't seen anyone who looked out of the ordinary, but then again, he wouldn't. He and the other Dragon Kings walked among the humans with no one the wiser. There was no reason it couldn't happen on Zora.

He stood and scrubbed a hand down his face. Time moved sluggishly. Thankfully, Tamlyn slept peacefully. She had been on edge *before* they arrived in Stonemore. What they'd discovered today only made things worse. He wished now that they hadn't left the ruins. Anyone could be an enemy here.

The problem was, he wasn't the only target. Cullen not only had to think about himself, he also had to consider Tamlyn. As the minutes ticked by and midnight came and went, he readied himself. The priests would bring the children out to sacrifice, and Tamlyn's power would take over. He had a plan. It was a good one, too. One that would go off perfectly if it weren't for whoever was after him.

He knew it wasn't the priests or the soldiers. It was someone with magic, targeting him and other dragons. That person or persons was hiding in the city, just as he was. They didn't wish to be caught any more than he did. Not that it would help in his escape plan for all of them, because he knew Tamlyn wouldn't leave even one child behind.

Cullen cracked his knuckles then tipped his neck side to side to loosen it. Eurwen had said she'd heard a voice but didn't see anything or anyone. She'd said whatever it was, was invisible. Cullen knew that some beings had such power. Larena, a female Warrior at MacLeod Castle, had such a gift. Who was to say there wasn't a Dragon King who had it?

What bothered him was how none of them knew. Surely, at least Con would've known about any new Kings—or even Queens. Then again, none of them had known about Brandr or Eurwen—or even Zora.

Fuck. Did that mean there were more Dragon Kings on Zora that no one, not even the twins, knew about? That would explain why dragons had been targeted, and why the twins had been struck.

But Cullen needed to keep one thing in mind. They were on a new realm. Granted, it looked and acted like Earth, but it wasn't. There were other magical beings here that weren't on his realm—like Tamlyn. Then there was the arrival of the human infants, all different races, just appearing out of nowhere.

It could be a Dragon King attacking them. Or it could be another entity altogether.

Cullen walked to the window and looked out over the city. Most windows were dark, but a few had lights on. His gaze scanned the buildings, wondering who was inside each structure. His enemy lurked somewhere, just out of sight.

He wasn't frightened. He and his brethren had fought and won against a group who called themselves the Others and had tried to rid Earth of the Kings. The Others hadn't succeeded. Whoever this was wouldn't either.

There was one difference, however. On Earth, the Kings battled as one. Cullen was alone in Stonemore. Not that he feared facing whoever— or whatever—was after him. Quite the opposite. What concerned him was that his findings wouldn't make it to his friends. If something happened to him, he wanted the Kings to know what he had uncovered. That would help them end this new foe.

Movement on the bed caught his attention. He turned and looked at Tamlyn over his shoulder. She was his mate. And there was a good chance he would lose her before she was ever really his. He hadn't told her of his feelings. To be fair, he hadn't realized them until a short time ago. With everything else she had on her plate, how could he add something else? Tamlyn was strong, but people could only take so much before they buckled. He didn't want to put her in that spot. Especially now.

He was turning back to the window when her body went rigid. Cullen went to the bed, and he looked down to find Tamlyn's eyes open and staring at the ceiling. Gone were her hazel eyes, now replaced by milky white ones.

Her hands jerked up and clutched her head as she rolled onto her side into a ball, her face creased with pain. He started to touch her, then thought better of it. Suddenly, she was on her feet and walking to the door. Cullen moved ahead of her to block her path.

"Move," she demanded.

He stared into her white eyes. "I need to know it's you."

Her brows drew together for a heartbeat. "Of course, it's me. But you need to get out of the way."

"Have you ever seen yourself after hearing the screams in your head?"

She gave him a quizzical look. "Why would I?"

Cullen produced a mirror and enough light for her to see. He watched the shock move across her face as she stared at herself.

She reached up and touched the outside corner of one eye. "Jenefer and Sian never said."

"I doona think they know. I didna see this last night. Only now."

Tamlyn looked up at him. "We have to go. Now."

He made the light and mirror disappear along with the image of the town. Then they quietly left the chamber and made their way down the hall to the stairs. The boards creaked as they descended the steps, but no one came out to see what was going on. The tavern itself was empty and silent. Cullen led the way to the door, but at the last moment, changed his mind. He grabbed Tamlyn's hand and led her around the bar to the back of the tavern.

Just as he expected, there was another door. They made their exit without encountering anyone. Once on the street, they pressed up against the building and listened. Most had found their beds, but like all cities, some favored the night. Those souls milled about, talking and laughing.

A man so drunk he could barely stand had his arm around a woman who was smiling and laughing as she led him down the street to a seedier tavern. No doubt she would fleece him of whatever coin he had, but that wasn't Cullen's concern.

When it was clear, he and Tamlyn made their way to the stairs. Once more, he led the way in case they encountered any soldiers. On the fourth level, Tamlyn jerked him to a stop. He moved them to an area in the shadows.

"What is it?" he whispered.

She jerked her chin down the road. "There are more guards than usual."

"They're prepared. I would've done the same."

She sighed. "How do we get past them?"

"Like everyone else."

Her eyes widened. "Is there another way?"

He wound his arm around her shoulders and leaned on her before stumbling into the light. Her arms came up to steady him. Cullen mumbled incoherently, slurring. To Tamlyn's credit, she didn't hesitate to take on her role. She cooed softly to him, cajoling and bribing him to go to the tavern.

Cullen heard the soldiers they passed chuckle. One said, "Poor sod."

When they finally made it to the tavern, Tamlyn led him beside it where the shadows could take them.

"Good job," he told her with a wink.

She flattened her lips. "It scared the hell out of me. Though it was a little fun."

They shared a smile. They had gotten through one part, but there was still more to go.

"Ready?"

"As I'll ever be," she murmured.

He waited until the guards looked away before the two of them moved away from the pub. The problem with getting to the temple was that few people, other than the soldiers, were nearby. And by few, he meant none.

"I've got an idea," he said as he came to a halt.

Tamlyn looked up at him expectantly.

"This," he said as he used magic to put them in soldier uniforms.

Her eyes rounded in surprise. "Will it work?"

"Let's find out."

This time when they walked, Cullen didn't keep to the shadows. They made their way to the temple, nodding to the small group of soldiers they passed. It was almost too easy to get to the temple.

"The children should be kept in the same room," Tamlyn told him as they walked to the temple's outside wall.

He glanced over the edge of the fourth level to see the sheer drop to the boulders below. Cullen almost asked how many times she had slipped, but he realized it was better if he didn't know.

"What if someone sees you?" she asked.

Cullen shrugged. "It's the chance you always take."

"True, but there were never this many soldiers about before."

There was likely more up top with the bairns, too, but he didn't tell her that. He couldn't chance going through the temple itself. He knew nothing of the inner workings of the priests or soldiers, which left this as their only option.

Cullen returned his clothes from before since it would be awkward to climb in armor. The clouds kept the moon hidden, but all it would take was one soldier looking up. He took a deep breath and jumped. He landed near the window and grasped one of the handholds he'd seen. From there, he quickly climbed the last few feet. He didn't like being so exposed where anyone could look up and see him.

When Cullen reached the window, he slowly lifted himself to peer inside. There was a group of children ranging in age from three to about six. Three soldiers surrounded them, with a priest kneeling in front of an altar at the back of the room. The children were red-eyed, their faces wet with tears as they sat huddled together. Fury consumed Cullen that anyone could do this to kids. He'd expected there to be soldiers, and he was glad of it because he wanted to take his anger out on those who deserved it.

He used his magic to silently open the window. Then he launched himself inside the room. Cullen punched the first soldier, knocking him out cold. He kicked the second into the wall and heard the crunch of bone. The third soldier came at him with a sword. Cullen easily took it from him and impaled the man. Cullen withdrew the blade and turned to the priest, who glared at him.

"You have no idea what you've done," the priest declared as he climbed to his feet.

Cullen nearly choked on the hatred within him. He didn't bother to hide his accent when he said, "I have an idea."

The priest snorted in derision. "You will die for interfering."

Cullen shook his head. "I'm not the one dying tonight. You should be protecting the children, not hurting them."

"They are the spawn of evil," the priest spat. "They need to be destroyed."

"Perhaps you should look in the mirror if you want to know evil."

The priest opened his mouth to scream. Cullen swung the blade with a speed only a Dragon King possessed. The priest grabbed at the wound as blood poured through his fingers. Cullen turned away before the priest hit the floor, sickened by the words he'd heard. How many children had been sacrificed because of those beliefs? How many had lost their lives because narrow-minded individuals couldn't see how petty, evil, and immoral they were?

He took a deep breath and focused on the children. They stared at him with wide eyes, filled with fear and uncertainty. A glance down showed that he was covered in blood. He slowly crouched and set aside the sword. Cullen smiled at each one. "I'm here to free all of you. My friend, Tamlyn, is at the bottom waiting so we can take you all to freedom."

At first, the children wouldn't move. Their fear was too great.

Cullen removed the blood from himself then held out his hand and produced a rope so they could see that he had magic. He nodded to them as he tied the rope around a column and let the rest drop outside the window. "You willna fall. Because I willna let you."

One of the girls jumped up first. She met his gaze and nodded. The innocence was gone from her blue eyes. Staring back at him was an adult in a child's body. It made him want to kill the priest and soldiers all over again.

Once Cullen had the girl outside the window and descending the rope, the others quickly lined up for their turn.

Chapter Twenty-two

A breath rushed past Tamlyn's lips when she saw the first child coming down the rope. She blinked back tears. It didn't matter to her that she hadn't been the one to get them out. What mattered was that they were free.

Tamlyn helped the girl to the ground. She smiled at the child, though wasn't disheartened when she didn't get one in return. Tamlyn pointed to the shadows. "Stay there, out of sight."

One by one, three more children came down the rope. She looked up, wondering where the fifth was. Tamlyn saw Cullen leaning his head out the window. Then the rope vanished from her hand. She hurried the children aside when she saw Cullen gather the last child in his arms and swing his legs out the window.

In the next breath, he landed beside her, holding the little girl in his arms. The child had a death grip on him. Tamlyn tried to take her, but the girl held on tighter.

"I've got her," Cullen whispered as his clothing once more changed into that of a soldier.

Tamlyn glanced at the children. They all looked traumatized. It made her thankful that she couldn't remember her time in the temple. Hopefully, those memories would fade for these children, too.

She leaned down to get even with their faces. "We're going to leave the city. We have to do it quietly. Don't make a sound."

"We'll be staying out of sight of everyone," Cullen told them. "We'll move fast to stay hidden. Tamlyn will take the lead, and I'll bring up the rear."

The children clustered together and waited. Tamlyn hesitated. She and Cullen had gotten there by dressing as soldiers. How would they get back with children in tow?

As if sensing her question, Cullen winked at her and whispered,

"Trust me."

She hated not knowing the plan, but it wouldn't matter if they planned this out. Rescues had to be fluid because many things could crop up or go wrong—as they had already discovered that night. But he had not only gotten them to the temple, Cullen had also liberated the children. Now, it was just getting out of Stonemore.

"My mummy didn't want me," the girl Cullen held murmured.

Cullen's arms tightened around her. "She couldna see how special you are. I do, lass."

The child straightened and placed a kiss on Cullen's cheek, causing Tamlyn's eyes to tear up. Seeing him holding the girl caused her heart to melt. Their gazes met. She had the overwhelming urge to kiss him and never let him go. It was a silly thought. He was a Dragon King and couldn't stay on her land, just as she could never go to his.

"Get ready for some mist," Cullen warned the children.

He drew in a great breath. When he released it, fog fell from his lips. The same fog from the first day she had met him, and the forest the night before. His eyes twinkled as he watched her.

"Stay with me," she told the kids as she took the hand of the girl nearest her.

They all linked hands, the last one taking Cullen's as the mist spread up, down, and out, covering the city. It was so thick that she could barely see in front of her, but she knew where she was headed. She walked quickly, intent on getting out of the city with all five children.

Tamlyn had barely exited the narrow alley when she saw a glint of armor through the fog. She slowed her steps as she tried to see what was in front of her. Suddenly, Cullen was there, handing her the little girl.

"There's a line of the priests' soldiers," he whispered.

She looked around him but couldn't see anything. "What do we do?"

"I'm going to make a distraction."

Her heart skipped a beat. She grabbed his arm. "Cullen, no. You need to come with us."

"The only way this will work is if I do this."

"No."

He gently touched her face. "I'll see you again. There's much left to say between us, lass. I'll do what I must so you can get the children and yourself out."

The only way he could cause a distraction was with magic. Tamlyn was terrified to ask if he would shift or do some other kind of magic. A part of her wanted him to shift so she could see him in all his dragon glory.

Then she had a thought. "What about the one following you?"

"It'll draw them out."

"I don't like this."

He gave her a quick, hard kiss. "Trust me."

"I do."

The little girl in her arms turned and touched Cullen's face. Tamlyn's eyes welled up with tears. She barely kept them in check when he kissed the back of the girl's hand and winked at her.

"Doona fear me," he warned the kids. "No matter what you see, I'm your friend."

That's when she knew he was going to shift. She was both panicked and excited.

He stepped back, holding her gaze. The fog moved away from him as if allowing their small group to see him. In the next instant, a dragon stood before her. The children gasped and moved closer to her, but they couldn't take their eyes from him.

Neither could she.

Tamlyn had never seen a dragon up close. She had barely seen one in the distance. Her lips parted in surprise at the sight of Cullen in his true form. He was enormous. He towered as high as the temple, his body barely contained in the courtyard. Thick, metallic scales in a stunning shade of garnet covered him with those on his belly shaded darker. His deep-set, turquoise-colored eyes watched her carefully. His head was bony and scaled, giving him a savage appearance, but she wasn't scared. Atop his skull was one central horn that spiraled up. A row of smaller horns ran along each side of his head and jaw. His nose was flat and had two long, pointy nostrils with small tendrils on his chin. A few large teeth poked from beneath his top lip. His wide neck ran to a bulky body with four limbs. Each limb had four digits that ended in long, onyx claws.

He stretched out his head to her. Tamlyn reached out a hand and laid it upon his nose and smiled at him. To her surprise, the children also touched him. The girl in her arms kissed her palm before placing it on Cullen's nose.

They remained a heartbeat more before he pulled back and gave her a nod. She swallowed, fearful of what might happen to him. His actions could bring about the war he'd vowed not to start.

Suddenly, he spread his colossal wings. They seemed to glow with fire itself. She stumbled back as she saw that spiked scales covered the tops of each visible bone. With a flap of his wings, the mist curled around him, clinging for a moment before falling away. She watched, stunned, as he raised his head and let out a roar that shook the mountain.

Then he was in the air, his long tail trailing behind him. He looked down at her before flying over the city. Chaos erupted all around her as people screamed and ran in panic. Tamlyn set the little girl on her feet.

"Grab hands," she yelled over the sound of the townspeople. "Stay close together."

With a child's hand in each of hers, she ran through the line of soldiers. They had their gazes skyward and never saw her.

* * * *

Cullen kept his eyes on Tamlyn and the bairns. He was the distraction they needed to make a clean getaway. He tipped his wing and swung back around. As he did, he passed close to the palace. Soldiers came rushing out, firing arrows. They all bounced off his scales. He briefly thought about releasing dragon fire on the palace but decided against it since he was already breaking promises by showing his true self.

Besides, he didn't know if the ruler was responsible for the child sacrifices, or if the priests ruled the city. It appeared as if it were the priests, but Cullen couldn't be sure of that from the little time he'd spent there.

He did another pass over the city. Tamlyn and the kids were now on the third level. She wasn't far from the stairs, leading to the second. Cullen would remain until they were in the forest. After what he'd come to learn in his time with Tamlyn, he shouldn't be shocked at the terror that ran through the city like wildfire at the sight of him.

His mere appearance caused pandemonium. He hadn't doused anyone with dragon fire. He hadn't attacked. He'd simply flown around the city. But the humans' terror was very real. Whatever they had been told about dragons caused anxiety and panic on a level Cullen had never witnessed before.

He found Tamlyn once more. They were on the second level. One more to go to freedom. The thought had barely registered when he saw something out of the corner of his eye. His instincts told him to turn at that instant. Something grazed him. That small contact disoriented him, causing his body to stiffen and freeze for a heartbeat.

He swung around, searching for who or what had attacked him. Just as before, he saw nothing. But he knew it was there. Waiting for the opportunity to strike again.

* * * *

Tamlyn glanced up at Cullen. The sound of his wings was reassuring. She tripped and hurriedly righted herself, when she saw a shudder run through Cullen's body, and the way he quickly turned around with fury in his eyes, she knew he had been attacked. The arrows being fired at him did nothing, so this had to be the enemy he searched for.

He had put himself in danger to help her and the children. If she hadn't already thought him perfect, he was then. And she would tell him as much the next time she saw. She didn't allow herself to consider that it might not be a possibility. It had to be.

Her grip on the children tightened when a group of people rushed through the streets, fighting each other, their fear, and the fog. She shoved her shoulder into someone who had pushed one of the kids to the ground. Tamlyn had to release her hold on the two children to get the other up before he was trampled. She did it with the help of the children.

No one seemed to care that there were kids about. They only cared about themselves. She spied a toddler crying in the streets when the fog cleared slightly. Tamlyn watched as people rushed by the boy, knocking him to the ground. No one helped him, no one stopped. She maneuvered their group to the toddler and lifted him into her arms. He shook as he clung to her, snot and tears covering his face.

She looked to the oldest girl. "Help me keep the others together."

The girl nodded as she stayed close to Tamlyn. It felt like an eternity weaving through the throng of people while keeping their small group together. They were jostled, hit, shoved, and run over. But they stayed together. The mist hid them, but it also hindered her sight. She wouldn't complain since Cullen had used his power to help her. She just wished he was there because he could see through it.

Eventually, they reached the stairs. Tamlyn paused to catch her breath. She was sweating, and her senses were on overload. She was hyperaware of every sound and movement. Adrenaline and resolve kept her on her feet and moving. A glance at the children told her they were hanging on by a thread. She gave them a nod and a smile she hoped looked better than it felt.

She took a deep breath and fell in with the crowd once more. It was just a few steps to the stairs that would take her to the ground level. The instant she saw the stairwell, she jerked to a stop and pulled the kids back. It was crowded with people who pushed and shoved, knocking others to the floor and walking over them. There was no way she could take the kids there. Her only other option was to remain on the road and take the long way to the gates, but at least that was safer than the steps.

"Come on," she called.

The kids clustered around her. She adjusted the toddler on her hip. Cullen passed over her, the beat of his wings stirring the air. That second of cool air soothed her enough to keep going.

They hadn't gone another twenty feet when she heard a shout ahead. The people in front of her abruptly halted and spun around, rushing back toward her. She had little time to shove the children out of the way before they were all crushed. Tamlyn kept the kids from following the others. She didn't know what'd caused the crowd to turn around, but they couldn't go back. Their way out was down, and that was where she would go.

When she was finally able, she looked ahead. The fog was dissipating. It still clung in patches, but it wasn't as thick as before, which allowed her to see the army who stood shoulder to shoulder across the road. Tamlyn glanced over her shoulder at the stairway, and just as she feared, people were coming back up that way, as well.

"Shite," she murmured.

Tamlyn looked skyward and saw Cullen's dark shape flying near the top of the mountain. She almost called for him but held back at the last minute. He was doing all he could. It would be wrong to ask for more. She would have to find a way out herself.

Six pairs of eyes watched her, waiting for her decision. Never had so much rested on her shoulders. They could go back up with the others, but what would that do? Nothing. They could remain where they were, which would get them caught. Or...they could make a run for the stairs to the lower level.

It was her only course of action. She was resourceful. She'd think of something.

"I hope," she whispered as she started toward the stairs.

"You there!" a voice bellowed. "Halt!"

Tamlyn pushed the kids. "Keep going."

"I said halt!"

Chapter Twenty-three

His enemy was still there. Cullen could sense it, even if he couldn't see them. If a glancing blow had caused him to shudder so painfully, what would a direct hit do? He didn't want to find out. But he had to know if it was something that could kill a King. Was another Dragon King out there, created by this new realm?

Or was it another entity entirely, hell-bent on killing dragons?

Neither scenario was a good one. Cullen remained in the air, continuing to circle the city. No matter how close he came to the palace, he had seen only soldiers. But what concerned him was that the army refused to open the gates to let people out. He didn't think too much of it, because Tamlyn had another way out.

At least he thought that until he saw the army gathering on the bottom two levels, preventing anyone from leaving. His gaze found Tamlyn with the children. To his surprise, she had another bairn on her hip. The soldiers had spotted her and were calling out to her.

Cullen readied himself to let out a roar when he saw a shimmer of something out of the corner of his eye again. This time, he tucked his wings and dove toward the city. He spread his wings, soaring over the tops of buildings on the third level. He'd managed to dodge another hit, but how many more would he see?

"*Con!*" he called through the mental link, hoping that, somehow, he could reach the other Kings and alert them. "*Vaughn! Anyone?*"

* * * *

Tamlyn grabbed the kids and hurriedly backed up when the soldiers rushed up from the stairway with their weapons drawn and pointed at them. She put her hand in front of the children to protect them—for what good it did.

She glared at the soldiers who blocked her path to the stairs. Behind her were more of the army, intending to keep her from reaching the gates. She kept turning, trying to keep everyone within view. A child's startled scream jerked her around.

A soldier had grabbed one of the children. He held a sword to the girl's neck, his fingers biting painfully into her shoulder to keep her still.

"Take off our armor, you thief," a soldier told her.

But she wasn't listening. Something inside her had changed. Like a switch had been flipped. Everything began to move in slow motion. She saw spittle fly from a soldier's mouth as he shouted. A bead of blood welled on the neck of the girl in the soldier's hold. Tamlyn watched as it rolled slowly down her skin.

Tamlyn looked to the child closest to her and gently pushed him down to the ground while the boy on her hip buried his face in her neck. She carefully placed him down, too. Rage and indignation were hurled at her in all directions. She looked down at her hands and saw them turning as if to gather the hateful emotions. The moment she did, a surge went through her. That's when she felt the scream begin to rise inside her. There was no fear, no trepidation. Somehow, she had found herself.

Tamlyn focused on the group of men closest to her, including the one who held the child. She drew in a deep breath and released the scream. The soldiers flew backwards. She grabbed hold of the girl and brought her close. Tamlyn looked at the men, who now lay unmoving. She didn't know if they were dead or unconscious—and she didn't care.

Behind her, she heard the other soldiers getting ready to attack. Tamlyn turned, urging the girl down like the rest of the children. The world still moved slowly as she faced the army. She watched in amazement as they charged her, uncaring or unfazed at what she had just done to their comrades.

Another scream welled within her. She let it build, waiting until she couldn't contain it, and then released it. The force of it knocked the men back as if an explosion had struck them.

In the silence that followed, time righted itself. Tamlyn gasped in a breath as she took in the scene before her. She turned in a circle and found the street empty, and the city quiet. She didn't stick around to find out what would happen.

"Come on," she urged the children.

They jumped to their feet and rushed to the stairway.

* * * *

Cullen wanted to shout with joy, even as he felt the shockwave of Tamlyn's scream. To witness her discovering her powers was glorious. He couldn't wait to celebrate with her. Maybe then he would tell her that she was his mate.

As much as he wanted to keep thinking about her, he returned his mind to whoever was after him. There hadn't been another attack, but he wasn't letting his guard down. It was out there watching and waiting for him to make a mistake. Cullen wanted to find the bastard, but he needed to safeguard Tamlyn and the bairns first. Then he'd return to find the wanker.

He looked down in time to see Tamlyn use her Banshee scream to burst open the city's gates and take out more soldiers. She walked out with her head held high and the kids by her side. Cullen turned and flew toward the forest.

As he spread his wings and soared over the city, he saw people begin filling the streets once more as they headed toward the gates that barely hung on their hinges. He smiled and looked for a place in the forest to land so he could meet up with Tamlyn.

He'd let his guard down, which was why he never saw the attack.

* * * *

Tamlyn couldn't contain her smile as she hurried from the city. The beat of Cullen's wings caught her attention. She looked up to see him flying over the forest. Her pace quickened. The children broke into a run to keep up with her.

The startled roar brought her to a sudden halt. The darkness prevented her from seeing anything. The crash of trees and the rumble of the ground beneath her feet told her all she needed to know.

"Cullen," she whispered, her heart hammering in her chest.

"Where's my dragon?" the little girl Cullen had jumped from the temple with asked.

Tamlyn glanced at her, then looked through the forest. She had to get to him. She jerked off the heavy armor, squared her shoulders, and walked into the forest. She kept to the road, her gaze darting about for any beasts coming to investigate the noises from Stonemore.

"He's out there," Tamlyn answered the child. "Waiting for us."

He'd been beside her every step of this endeavor. She couldn't imagine a day without him. She didn't *want* to imagine it. Ever. The thought of him gone from her life was devastating. He'd shown her how to embrace who she was. Without him, she might never have known she had such power within her. She certainly wouldn't have gone into Stonemore as they had.

His fearlessness and confidence showed her that it was okay to be afraid and when to take a stand. He methodically thought through any problem and came up with several solutions. He'd known from the beginning they would get separated. He'd warned her, but she hadn't wanted to listen because she hadn't thought she could do this alone.

While he'd known she *could*.

No one had ever had that kind of faith in her. Discovering that she was strong, that she had powers as a Banshee, allowed her to shake off her past that haunted her. She still had a long way to go, but it was a start she'd not had before.

Tamlyn switched the toddler to her other hip as tears welled. Cullen was an immortal. He couldn't be hurt. He couldn't.

But she'd heard a crash, one that sounded like something large falling to the ground. Something large like a dragon? She didn't want to think about it, but she couldn't think of anything else.

* * * *

Cullen stared up at the sky through human eyes as he fought to catch his breath after his fall. He rolled onto his hands and knees and took stock of his body. Everything hurt. His muscles twitched erratically, and his bones ached as if they had been pulled apart. The wound on his back where he'd been struck had already healed, but remnants of the magic remained.

He took in several breaths, trying to get the world to stop spinning. When it did, he saw that he had decimated the area around him. Trees were splintered, others flattened. He managed to get to his feet as he called clothes to him. He weaved slightly while turning around to look for his attacker.

This wasn't the first time he'd been struck down, but he'd never experienced anything like this. Dark Fae magic wasn't as painful as this. Whatever power this was, the Kings needed to learn of it immediately so they could protect themselves.

Cullen briefly closed his eyes. When he opened them, he saw something out of the corner of his eye again. This time, he remained still to see if he could get a better idea of what it was. He'd thought it a shimmer before, but he was wrong. It was more like a ripple through water.

"I know you're there," he told his foe.

Silence met his statement.

"Who are you? What do you want?"

"Your death."

The disembodied whisper seemed to come from all around him. Cullen tried to shift back into his true form. To his disbelief, he couldn't.

The laugh that filled the air set his teeth on edge.

Oh, yes, he was going to find this fucker and rip him apart. Cullen widened his stance and braced himself. He could battle in either form. If this bastard wanted a fight, Cullen would give him one.

Cullen used his peripheral vision to anticipate the attack. He saw it come at him from the left and dove out of the way. He didn't see the one from behind that sent him face-first into a splintered tree trunk. A shard the width of his hand impaled him through his shoulder.

There wasn't time to yank it out as he saw the ripple in the air come at him from the right again. This time, he predicted when the being would be upon him and drew up his fist. He thought he'd connect with something. Instead, his hand met air. Cullen was so stunned that he could only stare at his hand.

Suddenly, he was flung to the side, landing so the fragment of wood thrust deeper into his shoulder. Cullen jumped to his feet and bared his teeth.

"Afraid to face me? Only a coward attacks as you are."

The faceless voice laughed once more. "Only those being beaten say such things."

Cullen couldn't make out if the hoarse voice was male or female. What he did know was that whoever this was, they had no intention of showing their face. He saw the ripple once more and prepared to use magic to contain whoever it was.

When the being rushed him, the bushes nearby rustled as a wildcat jumped and landed before Cullen. The cat was clawing at something, growling and biting at what looked like air. Yet it was apparent the animal could see whatever the entity was. Just as quickly as the cat had attacked, it stopped and began licking its paws. After a few minutes, it looked up at Cullen sleepily and reclined on its side.

He stared at the animal in amazement. "What did you see?"

The animal yawned, showing off its many teeth. Its ears swiveled around to hear something behind them. The wildcat jumped up and trotted off without another look at Cullen. He watched the feline vanish into the forest.

"Cullen?"

He jerked at the sound of Tamlyn's voice. "I'm here," he said as he yanked the shard from his shoulder and ran to her.

Her smile was bright as she rushed him, wrapping her free arm around him. Cullen embraced her and smiled at the toddler, who seemed content to be in her arms.

"There's my dragon," a small voice declared.

He felt hands on his leg and looked down to see the little girl he'd carried. Cullen lifted her into his arms. She laid her head on his uninjured shoulder as he looked at the other four. Somehow, they had come out of a terrible situation.

"Have we had enough adventure for the night?" he asked.

Everyone nodded.

"Let's go home," Tamlyn said.

Home. Dreagan was his home. Or it had been. He wasn't sure anymore. A lot hinged on Tamlyn's response to being his mate.

His shoulder had healed, and there was only silence in the forest as they made their way to the other side. They were nearly out of the woods when he spotted Con, Brandr, Eurwen, and Vaughn walking toward them.

"Where the bloody hell have you been?" Vaughn demanded.

Cullen glanced at Tamlyn. "It's a long story that I'll be happy to tell once we have the bairns settled."

Eurwen smiled and held out her hand to the children. One of them walked slowly to her and hesitantly took her hand. Con squatted and motioned to one of the boys. The child was so exhausted that he fell into Con's arms and was asleep before the King straightened. Vaughn and Brandr each took another.

"This should be interesting," Tamlyn murmured as their group walked to the canyon.

Once there, Brandr and Eurwen teleported everyone to the bottom.

"Oh," Tamlyn said when she realized what had happened. "I could get used to that."

Eurwen smiled in response. Tamlyn led them to the hidden door and then inside the ruins. Cullen watched his friends' faces as they saw what was underground. He wasn't surprised to see Jenefer and Sian waiting at the bottom of the steps.

"Introductions after the children are settled," Tamlyn told her friends.

The group followed her down a corridor to a room where the other kids were. Cullen wasn't surprised to see them all together, despite the many rooms in the ruins. They likely felt safer that way.

"I stay with you," the girl in his arms said as she tightened her grip around his neck when Cullen tried to put her down.

He leaned back to look at her. "You need to rest."

"You my dragon."

His heart filled with love as he stared into her brown eyes. Cullen knelt next to the bedding and smoothed down her blond curls. "I'll be here, lass. You have my word."

Reluctantly, she nodded and loosened her hold. He gently laid her down and covered her with the blanket. She stared up at him solemnly. He couldn't imagine what she had been through, but he would make sure that she knew she was safe. He smiled and rested his hand against her cheek before standing.

At the door, he paused and looked back to find her gaze still on him. He waved and quietly walked out to join the others in the great hall, though a part of him wanted to bring the child. He'd liked having the girl with him. It wasn't that he didn't like children—he liked them a great deal. But he had resigned himself to never having any. What he hadn't counted on was his heart being stolen by a child who called him *her dragon*.

"There you are," Tamlyn said when he walked to their group.

He sensed the tension as Tamlyn stood between Jenefer and Sian while his friends stood across from them. Cullen paused between Jenefer and Brandr. He let his gaze move between the seven before taking a deep breath and motioning to Con, who was the farthest away. "Constantine, King of Dragon Kings, his daughter Eurwen, Vaughn, King of Teals and Eurwen's mate, and Brandr, brother to Eurwen." Cullen then motioned to his left. "This is Jenefer, an Amazon, Tamlyn a Banshee, and Sian, an

Alchemist."

"That was you we heard screaming, wasn't it?" Eurwen asked Tamlyn.

Sian's and Jenefer's heads jerked to Tamlyn in dismay as they asked in unison, "You screamed?"

"I did," Tamlyn replied. Her gaze moved to him. "It just happened."

"I saw it all from the sky. You were trapped, and your magic answered," Cullen explained.

"I want all the details," Sian stated.

Jenefer nodded, shock on her face. "Every detail, Tam."

Con's black eyes locked on him, anger simmering below the surface. "You were where?"

"It was to save the children and me," Tamlyn hurried to reply.

Cullen held Con's stare.

"You promised," Brandr stated furiously.

Eurwen sighed heavily. "Did you not hear Tamlyn? He didn't have a choice."

"There's always a choice," Brandr barked.

Cullen slid his gaze to him. "Really? Go into that room with the bairns and choose which one I should've let die? Or how about all of them? That isna who I am. I created a distraction. That's all."

"Let's hope that's all," Vaughn said.

Jenefer nodded. "I appreciate Tamlyn and the kids getting back, but I'm worried, too."

"I'm more concerned with why Cullen fell as if he was attacked."

He winced at Tamlyn's words, though he should've known she would say something.

"It might be dark outside, but I saw the blood on your clothes and the rip in your shoulder," Tamlyn said, pointing to the now-healed wound.

Cullen rubbed his hand on the back of his neck and looked at his friends. "Much happened in a short time while we were in Stonemore. Let's get comfortable so Tamlyn and I can tell all of you."

Brandr moved back a few paces, snapped his fingers so a fire roared between them, and then lowered himself to the floor. "I'm comfortable."

Cullen bit back the retort on his lips. There was much about him that reminded Cullen of Con. And Rhi. Brandr had Con's penetrating look down, but he also had Rhi's assertiveness. Cullen had to remind himself that Brandr and Eurwen were in charge of this realm, not him, Con, or any of the other Dragon Kings.

And that was hard to swallow.

They all found seating. Then he and Tamlyn began their tale. When they finished, six pairs of eyes stared at them with shock, elation, and fury.

"I would've loved to see the priests get what they deserved," Sian said with a smile.

Con was still. *Too* still, as he stared at Cullen.

"I always knew you had it in you," Jenefer told Tamlyn.

Vaughn briefly closed his eyes and lifted a hand in front of him. "Cullen. You knew someone had broken your communication and you stayed?"

"It wasn't as if he had a choice," Eurwen said.

Jenefer snorted and said to Eurwen, "I notice that you seem to be the voice of reason with these males."

"I understand what they're feeling because I feel it, too. But I want more answers." Eurwen's silver gaze landed on him.

Cullen sighed. "You're right. I didna have a choice. Tamlyn wouldna leave, and I wasna going to go just because I couldna get in touch with any of you."

"Need I remind you what happened to Varek?" Vaughn asked.

Cullen shook his head slowly. "His being brought here had nothing to do with the enemy we seek."

"You doona know that," Brandr said.

Con still stared at him without saying a word. That was never a good sign.

Eurwen caught his gaze. "You said you never saw the enemy?"

"I caught movement out of the corner of my eye. Like ripples."

Brandr's lips flattened. "I saw something similar before I was attacked."

"As did I," Eurwen admitted.

Vaughn's frown deepened. "Nothing head-on?"

Cullen shook his head. "I was getting my arse soundly kicked when the wildcat arrived. It could see whatever attacked me. Had the wildcat not leapt on it, I'd probably still be fighting it."

"This invisible adversary didna strike you as it did Eurwen, Brandr, or the other dragons?" Vaughn asked.

"I think it tried. I managed to dodge a few, but I was grazed with something as I flew over the forest. That's why I fell. My entire body seized."

Eurwen wrapped her arms around herself. "You can't move."

"No matter how much you want to," Brandr said.

Jenefer looked between them. "Are you saying this thing is invisible and attacks dragons?"

"Aye," Cullen replied.

Tamlyn was pale, her eyes large in her face as she stared at him. "How long until this thing starts going after the rest of us?"

"Depends on what it wants." Con's voice filled the silence.

Chapter Twenty-four

First one Dragon King, then three more. And a Dragon Queen? Tamlyn could hardly believe her eyes. She'd dreaded the dragons for so long. They were still fearsome creatures, but she'd also discovered they could be friendly.

Her gaze moved to Cullen. She had tuned out the debate he was having with the others about what had attacked him. She hadn't realized how close to harm he had actually come. Cullen had proven time and again that he was a man of his word. He had protected her, guided her, and steered her to understanding who she really was. For that alone, she would never be able to thank him.

There was so much she wanted to say to him. Alone. She understood that things needed to be settled with everyone, but she was beginning to think the current discussion would go on for hours.

She stifled a yawn. Now that everyone was safe, and her adrenaline had waned, she was having a hard time keeping her eyes open. She blinked several times, trying to wake herself. All she managed was to bring on another yawn.

Sian and Jenefer were completely absorbed in the discussion. Frankly, Tamlyn was a little surprised by Sian. Her mind was usually occupied with new creations in her lab. Yet, she had remained through the entirety of the story and the subsequent discussion. Ordinarily, Sian couldn't be bothered with such things.

Then again, things had changed for all of them.

Tamlyn inwardly berated herself. She didn't know why Sian's interest rubbed her wrong. Maybe she was just tired of waiting for the talk to be finished so she could catch Cullen's attention. Tamlyn covered her hand with her mouth as another yawn took her. She was having a difficult time keeping her eyes open. If she wanted to remain alert, she needed to stand and move around to get the blood flowing.

No one paid her any heed when she quietly got up and walked in the direction of the kitchen. Her stomach rumbled, causing her to smile and think of the pizza she had eaten. She wanted more of it. Hopefully, she wouldn't have to wait too long.

She paused to look in on the children on her way. Most were asleep, though some were simply lying silently. She smiled at them and walked to the kitchen. Once there, she looked around but didn't want anything. Her thoughts were on Cullen. Was his mission finished? Would he return to dragon land? Or worse, his realm? What about their time together?

As much as she wanted more time with him, she couldn't imagine how it would work. She couldn't go to his side of the boundary, and he couldn't remain here. Where did that leave them? The thought left her with an ache in her chest. Because she had developed feelings for him. Deep ones. The kind that involved her heart.

"Tamlyn?"

She whirled around at the sound of Cullen's voice.

He wore a frown as he walked to her. "Are you all right?"

"I'm just feeling a little worn out."

A blond brow quirked. "Is that all?"

"Mostly."

"You can tell me anything. You know that, right?"

Knowing she could and actually doing it were two different things. "Yes."

"Then what's holding you back?"

Everything. But she wouldn't tell him that, either. Instead, she shrugged. "I don't know where to begin."

"Then let me."

"W-what?" She hadn't expected that. She wasn't sure why not. Cullen had surprised her at every turn.

He grinned and reached for her hand. "Why are you shocked? Did I no' make my intentions evident?"

"I..." What could she say?

"Let me make my wishes clear then."

Only an idiot would say no to that, and she wasn't an idiot. "All right."

He took her hand and led her through the corridors. It wasn't long before she realized he was taking her to the part of the ruins she had asked him to remain in when he first arrived. A smile pulled at her lips when he walked her into the very chamber she'd chosen for him.

The darkened room suddenly lit up from a source above them that hung in midair. She didn't need to ask to know that Cullen had done it.

"I want you to see my face," he told her as he faced her.

Tamlyn looked into his pale brown eyes and wanted to wrap her arms around him. She managed to contain herself. Barely.

Cullen cleared his throat and shifted his feet as if he were nervous. It bolstered her because she didn't think anything would make him anxious. Especially not her. But…perhaps his feelings did go deep. Maybe… If she dared to imagine the possibility.

"I've been alive for a long time," he began. "I've seen more than you can imagine and experienced so much that I've forgotten most of it. I've waged war and lived in peace. I've ruled thousands of Garnets, and I've suffered quietly alone in my mountain."

His words made her heart catch. No one should have to suffer alone. Ever. But she understood because *she* had suffered alone.

Cullen's gaze slid away briefly. "Some flout destiny. They scorn the idea of Fate. No' me. I've always trusted the path I was put on. I might have questioned it a few times, but I knew there was a purpose. I didna foresee that purpose being you. When I saw you running from the forest as dawn broke, I had the overwhelming urge to come to your defense. Even after, when I knew I should return to my side of the barrier, I couldna. I had to meet you, to see you. To talk to you. That still wasna enough."

This couldn't really be happening to her. Could it? If it was a dream, she hoped she never woke.

"I would've defied orders to help you," Cullen continued. "I didna care who tried to stop me or why. That was how compelled I was to return to your side. And I doona wish to leave it now. Or ever."

Her lips parted, but no words came. In all her imaginings, she hadn't dared to allow herself to believe that Cullen felt such things for her. She swallowed, the sound loud in the silence. What did she say? How did she answer? So many words were jumbled in her mind that she couldn't manage to string a sentence together.

"Of course, if you doona feel the same, tell me," Cullen said. "I know you felt something when we shared our bodies. But it might be too soon for yo—"

Tamlyn put a finger over his lips to quiet him. She saw the uncertainty in his eyes. This man, this Dragon King, had laid bare his heart. To her. If she hadn't already been in love with him, she would've fallen for him right then.

"Shhh," she said with a smile and let her hand drop to her side. "I was so surprised by your words that I was left speechless for a moment." He had been honest with her. The least she could do was give him the same. She took a deep breath and looked into his eyes. "I've never encountered anyone like you. You shielded me at the same time you pushed me. You didn't try to hold me back but gave me the courage to do things I never would've done. You showed me what it was to be cherished. I never thought I was worthy of it."

His face contorted at her words as he brought their bodies together. "You are worthy, lass."

"You helped me see that. I found my true self, the Banshee I feared to be, because of you. You helped me find my strength and my power."

The back of his knuckles caressed her cheek. "You've always had it within you. You just needed a wee nudge."

"You say you don't want to leave me. I don't want to be without you."

His mouth came down on hers, the kiss passionate and full of love. Her arms wound around his neck as he held her firmly. He didn't end the kiss until both of them were breathing hard.

"You've made me so happy," he said.

She looked at him. "How? How can we do this?"

"We'll find a way. There's always a way. Fate wouldna have chosen you as my mate otherwise."

Tamlyn jerked back. "What?"

"Dragons mate for life," he explained. "We're able to sense when we've found our mates. You're mine."

"But...I'm not a dragon."

He grinned and gave her a quick kiss. "It's been a long time since a King has mated with another dragon."

"You found the dragons now. Wouldn't it make sense that you would find your mate with them?"

"Do you no' want me?"

"I didn't say that," she argued.

He took a deep breath and released it. "You're my mate. It's that simple. The rest…we'll work it out."

She hesitated.

"What is it?" he pressed.

"I want to be with you. It's just that I don't want to rush into anything."

He brought her against him, hugging her as he kissed her forehead. "Ah, lass. I'll no' push you to do anything you are no' ready for. This is enough for now. I love you."

She leaned back to look at him, her heart near to bursting. "And I love you."

Epilogue

The next day…

"I'm no' surprised," Con said as he and Cullen walked together from the ruins, the others behind them.

Cullen glanced at him. "About?"

"Tamlyn being your mate. Your attempt at no' getting close would only last for so long."

Cullen laughed and glanced over his shoulder at Tamlyn, who briefly met his gaze. "I didna want a mate, but it seemed destiny had other plans."

"That usually happens," Con said with a grin. It faded quickly. "I doona like leaving you over here alone. If you're right, our new enemy recognized you before you ever shifted. They'll be searching for you."

Cullen watched as Con jumped to the top of the canyon. He quickly followed and faced his King. "My staying makes the most sense. As much as I'd love to bring Tamlyn to our side, she willna go without her friends or the children. Also, after such a divide between cultures, it would be wrong to do that to the dragons."

"Things have no' been going as smoothly as we'd hoped with Jeyra there. The dragons doona seem to care that she's Varek's mate. They know her as human. It's why I have her and Varek on Earth for the time being." Con turned his head to look down the canyon at the others. Then his black eyes landed on him once more. "By remaining, we're breaking the rules that Eurwen and Brandr put in place. We're going to have to come up with some way to pacify both sides."

"Right now, the ruins work in our favor. They sprawl over both dragon and human land."

"Let's hope that works. At least the canyon is close to the barrier." Con's gaze swept the area. "Since our new foe is invisible, I can no' help but think they're watching."

Cullen nodded in agreement. "I've been wondering if it's a rogue King that the twins are no' aware of. This realm is so different from Earth. With the infants appearing out of nowhere, the humans unable to have bairns, and magical beings we doona have on our realm, anything is possible."

"I've thought of that. I spoke briefly with Brandr about it last night. He's sure there isna another King or Queen on the realm. He said they would've challenged him and Eurwen. I have to agree with that assessment."

"It's a possibility. Just as it could be some being we've never encountered before."

Con's face went hard. "One we can no' see."

A gasp to his right caught his attention. He turned to see that Eurwen and Brandr had teleported the others up to the rim of the canyon, but that wasn't what'd caused the reaction. He followed their gazes to the wildcat walking toward them.

"I'll be damned," Cullen said with a smile as he recognized the same big feline that had saved him.

He moved away from Con and waited for the animal to reach him. The wildcat butted its head against him. Cullen smoothed his hand over the cat's soft fur as it made grunting noises with its eyes closed. After a few more scratches, the cat made its way down the canyon and lay next to the doorway of the ruins, casually waiting on him. Cullen smiled as he realized that the cat was female.

"I sure hope he won't eat us," Sian said.

Cullen shook his head. "*She* willna. She's our friend."

"Let's hope so," Jenefer replied.

Eurwen rubbed her hands together. "I want to pet her."

"It would be great if you could use her to find our new foe," Brandr told Cullen.

Cullen met his gaze and grinned. "I was thinking of just that."

"I think you might need to check on Tamlyn," Con said with a frown.

Cullen whirled to his mate to find her eyes white. This time, however, she wasn't writhing in pain.

"She tripped and grabbed one of the stone faces on the way out," Jenefer explained.

Tamlyn slowly turned her head to Cullen, a smile splitting her face. "I know why I love this place so."

Cullen made his way to her. "What is it, love?"

A tear fell down her cheek. "It's called Iron Hall. It was built by Banshees. They continued to expand as they accepted everyone with magic."

"Where did they go?" Brandr asked.

Another tear. "I don't know. Something came for everyone here. They just...left."

Cullen exchanged a look with Con.

"We've left the humans to their own devices," Eurwen said. "We thought that was the answer. If we didn't bother them, they wouldn't bother us."

Brandr shrugged. "We can no' govern everyone."

"But something has to be done," Vaughn replied.

Jenefer put her hand on the hilt of her sword. "Sian, Tamlyn, and I have worked alone for years. We've managed a few victories, but it hasn't been easy. We thought it was better if we didn't get others involved in our quest, but I think that was the wrong decision."

Tamlyn blinked, her eyes returning to normal as she looked at Jenefer. "You want to find the other Amazons."

"I do." Jenefer looked at the dragons as if daring them to go against her.

Con jerked his chin to Iron Hall. "You have a safe place. Gather those you can trust. It's the only way your people will stop being victimized. It willna be easy. It will be a difficult road."

"But you won't be alone," Cullen said.

A muscle ticked in Brandr's jaw. "Doona promise what you can no' give," he warned Cullen.

Eurwen put her hand on her brother's arm. She held his gaze for a moment then looked at Jenefer, Sian, and Tamlyn. "We're friends now. We've set boundaries between our people and yours for a reason. If we join with you, it will start the war we've ensured would never happen."

"It's already played out on our realm," Vaughn said.

Con nodded slowly. "We willna allow a repeat here."

"Then what good is your friendship?" Jenefer asked.

Tamlyn jerked her head to her, astonishment on her face. "Jenefer!"

"It's a valid question," Eurwen replied.

Brandr sighed loudly. "As you know, someone is after us. Cullen remaining is our link to each other. If anything happens, cross the barrier. We have Kings patrolling the perimeter. They'll know what to do if they see any of you. Cullen can also get in contact with us, and we can return if we need to."

"Thank you," Jenefer said.

Cullen hid his smile at the relief on Sian's face.

They said their farewells. Con lingered for a moment longer. He said nothing, but he didn't have to. Cullen understood what the silence meant.

* * * *

They were finally alone. Tamlyn snuggled against Cullen as they lay on her new bed. Cullen had given everyone new beds. So much was possible with magic. She had magic now. It was different than Cullen's, but she had it. Something she'd never thought possible.

"I can't believe you stayed," she said.

He kissed the top of her head. "Things are complicated, but we can navigate them."

"Did you tell Con I was your mate?"

"I didna need to. He saw it. So did the others."

Tamlyn winced. "Are they okay with it?"

"We doona get to choose who our mates are, lass. They know that and accept it. What about you? Did you tell Sian and Jenefer?"

"I did."

Cullen chuckled. "I guess that brief answer speaks volumes."

"Sian is happy. Jenefer is hopeful about things but cautious."

"That's wise."

Tamlyn pushed up on her elbow. "What does it mean to be your mate, exactly?"

"There's a ceremony where we will be bound to each other."

"Like a wedding?"

He nodded. "Since dragons mate for life, it's important that you know what you're getting into. It's why I'm no' pushing for the ceremony."

"You'll live a lot longer than I will."

"Once the ceremony happens and we're joined, you will live as long as I do."

Her mouth went slack. "Are you serious?"

"Aye," he replied with a small grin.

"What if someone gets it wrong."

He looked away briefly. "Dragons doona get it wrong. On the off chance the couple no longer wishes to be together later, they will separate. For the human, she'll continue to be immortal as long as her King lives. She could go on and find a new love and life."

"What of the King?" Tamlyn asked.

"We can no' survive without our mate once we've found her. If she doesna want us, then eventually, we'll die without her."

Tamlyn looked deep into his eyes. "It's important that we get it right."

"Are you worried?"

"I know what I feel. The truth is that I've not spent much time with men. I need to get used to you," she said with a smile.

He laughed and pulled her down for a kiss. "We have all the time we need."

Tamlyn wanted to argue that point and remind him about the dragons' enemy, but his kiss deepened, and all she could think about was having him inside her.

* * * *

The series continues with DRAGON ETERNAL coming June 2022.

* * * *

Also from 1001 Dark Nights and Donna Grant, discover Dragon Revealed, Dragon Lost, Dragon Claimed, Dragon Night, Dragon Burn, Dragon Fever, and Dragon King.

Sign up for the 1001 Dark Nights Newsletter
and be entered to win a Tiffany Key necklace.

There's a contest every month!

Go to www.1001DarkNights.com to subscribe.

**As a bonus, all subscribers can download
FIVE FREE exclusive books!**

Discover 1001 Dark Nights Collection Nine

DRAGON UNBOUND by Donna Grant
A Dark Kings Novella

NOTHING BUT INK by Carrie Ann Ryan
A Montgomery Ink: Fort Collins Novella

THE MASTERMIND by Dylan Allen
A Rivers Wilde Novella

JUST ONE WISH by Carly Phillips
A Kingston Family Novella

BEHIND CLOSED DOORS by Skye Warren
A Rochester Novella

GOSSAMER IN THE DARKNESS by Kristen Ashley
A Fantasyland Novella

THE CLOSE-UP by Kennedy Ryan
A Hollywood Renaissance Novella

DELIGHTED by Lexi Blake
A Masters and Mercenaries Novella

THE GRAVESIDE BAR AND GRILL by Darynda Jones
A Charley Davidson Novella

THE ANTI-FAN AND THE IDOL by Rachel Van Dyken
A My Summer In Seoul Novella

A VAMPIRE'S KISS by Rebecca Zanetti
A Dark Protectors/Rebels Novella

CHARMED BY YOU by J. Kenner
A Stark Security Novella

HIDE AND SEEK by Laura Kaye
A Blasphemy Novella

DESCEND TO DARKNESS by Heather Graham
A Krewe of Hunters Novella

BOND OF PASSION by Larissa Ione
A Demonica Novella

JUST WHAT I NEEDED by Kylie Scott
A Stage Dive Novella

Also from Blue Box Press

THE BAIT by C.W. Gortner and M.J. Rose

THE FASHION ORPHANS by Randy Susan Meyers and M.J. Rose

TAKING THE LEAP by Kristen Ashley
A River Rain Novel

SAPPHIRE SUNSET by Christopher Rice writing C. Travis Rice
A Sapphire Cove Novel

THE WAR OF TWO QUEENS by Jennifer L. Armentrout
A Blood and Ash Novel

THE MURDERS AT FLEAT HOUSE BY Lucinda Riley

THE HEIST by C.W. Gortner and M.J. Rose

Discover More Donna Grant

Dragon Revealed
A Dragon Kings Novella

The capture of a Dragon King is cause for celebration. Jeyra never dreamed she would actually face one of the creatures who destroyed her home. But the longer she's around him, the more she finds herself gravitating to him. All it takes is one reckless kiss that unleashes desires and the truth that has been hidden from her to set them both on a course that could be the end of them.

Varek, King of Lichens, has known nothing but a life with magic. Until he finds himself on a different realm unable to call up his powers. Worse, he's in shackles with no memory of how it happened. When he sees an enthralling woman who leaves him speechless, he believes he can charm her to free him. The more she rebuffs him, the more he craves her, igniting a dangerous passion between them. Can he protect the woman he's fallen for while uncovering the truth – or will peril that neither see coming tear them apart?

* * * *

Dragon Lost
A Dark Kings Novella

Destinies can't be ignored. No one knows that better than Annita. For as long as she can remember, it's been foretold she would find a dragon. A real-life dragon. She's beginning to think it was all some kind of mistake until she's swimming in one of the many caves around the island and discovers none other than a dragon. There is no fear as she approaches, utterly transfixed at the sight of the creature. Then he shifts into the shape of a thoroughly gorgeous man who spears her with bright blue eyes. In that instant, she knows her destiny has arrived. And the dragon holds the key to everything.

All Royden wanted was to find an item his brother buried when they were children. It was supposed to be a quick and simple trip, but he should've known nothing would be easy with enemies like the Dragon

Kings have. Royden has no choice but to trust the beguiling woman who tempts him like no other. And in doing so, they unleash a love so strong, so pure that nothing can hold it back.

* * * *

Dragon Claimed
A Dark Kings Novella

Born to rule the skies as a Dragon King with power and magic, Cináed hides his true identity in the mountains of Scotland with the rest of his brethren. But there is no respite for them as they protect the planet and the human occupants from threats. However, a new, more dangerous enemy has targeted the Kings. One that will stop at nothing until dragons are gone forever. But Cináed discovers a woman from a powerful, ancient Druid bloodline who might have a connection to this new foe.

Solitude is sanctuary for Gemma. Her young life was upended one stormy night when her family disappears, leaving her utterly alone. She learned to depend solely on herself from then on. But no matter where she goes she feels…lost. As if she missed the path she was supposed to take. Everything changes when she backs into the most dangerously seductive man she's ever laid eyes. Gemma surrenders to the all-consuming attraction and the wild, impossible love that could destroy them both – and finds her path amid magic and dragons.

* * * *

Dragon Night
A Dark Kings Novella

Governed by honor and ruled by desire

There has never been a hunt that Dorian has lost. With his sights sent on a relic the Dragon Kings need to battle an ancient foe, he won't let anything stand in his way – especially not the beautiful owner. Alexandra is smart and cautious. Yet the attraction between them is impossible to deny – or ignore. But is it a road Dorian dares to travel down again?

With her vast family fortune, Alexandra Sheridan is never without suitors. No one is more surprised than she when the charming, devilish

Scotsman snags her attention. But the secrets Dorian holds is like a wall between them until one fateful night when he shares everything. In his arms she finds passion like no other – and a love that will transcend time. But can she give her heart to a dragon??

* * * *

Dragon Burn
A Dark Kings Novella

Marked by passion

A promise made eons ago sends Sebastian to Italy on the hunt to find an enemy. His quarry proves difficult to locate, but there is someone who can point him in the right direction – a woman as frigid as the north. Using every seductive skill he's acquired over his immortal life, his seduction begins. Until he discovers that the passion he stirs within her makes him burn for more…

Gianna Santini has one love in her life – work. A disastrous failed marriage was evidence enough to realize she was better off on her own. That is until a handsome Scot strolled into her life and literally swept her off her feet. She is unprepared for the blazing passion between them or the truth he exposes. But as her world begins to unravel, she realizes the only one she can depend on is the very one destroying everything - a Dragon King.

* * * *

Dragon Fever
A Dark Kings Novella

A yearning that won't be denied

Rachel Marek is a journalist with a plan. She intends to expose the truth about dragons to the world – and her target is within sight. Nothing matters but getting the truth, especially not the ruggedly handsome, roguishly thrilling Highlander who oozes danger and charm. And when she finds the truth that shatters her faith, she'll have to trust her heart to the very man who can crush it…

A legend in the flesh

Suave, dashing Asher is more than just a man. He's a Dragon King – a being who has roamed this planet since the beginning of time. With everything on the line, Asher must choose to trust an enemy in the form of an all too alluring woman whose tenacity and passion captivate him. Together, Asher and Rachel must fight for their lives – and their love – before an old enemy destroys them both…

* * * *

Dragon King
A Dark Kings Novella

A Woman on A Mission

Grace Clark has always done things safe. She's never colored outside of the law, but she has a book due and has found the perfect spot to break through her writer's block. Or so she thinks. Right up until Arian suddenly appears and tries to force her away from the mountain. Unaware of the war she just stumbled into, Grace doesn't just discover the perfect place to write, she finds Arian - the most gorgeous, enticing, mysterious man she's ever met.

A King with a Purpose

Arian is a Dragon King who has slept away centuries in his cave. Recently woken, he's about to leave his mountain to join his brethren in a war when he's alerted that someone has crossed onto Dreagan. He's ready to fight...until he sees the woman. She's innocent and mortal - and she sets his blood aflame. He recognizes the danger approaching her just as the dragon within him demands he claim her for his own...

Dark Alpha's Passion
Reaper Book 12
By Donna Grant
Coming March 8, 2022

From *New York Times* bestselling author Donna Grant comes another gripping story in her Reaper series featuring a brotherhood of elite assassins who wage war on the Fae at Death's behest—and the women who dare to love them.

There is no escaping a Reaper. I am an elite assassin, part of a brotherhood that only answers to Death. And when Death says your time is up, I'm coming for you...

The latest threat uncovered, it is my honor and duty to oust those responsible for the slaughter of so many and make the Fae Others pay for their crimes. However, nothing could have prepared me for the stunning and curious female that crosses my path. She's an enigma: equal parts strength and vulnerability. She quiets the rage I've carried within me for so long and makes me question Death's directives for the first time ever. Her tragic, emotional story touches something deep within me, and her bravery is awe-inspiring—which makes it doubly hard to let her return to the enemy and the dangers that await. I never expected her, but I need her. She is everything to me, and I will do whatever it takes to make sure she's safe and by my side. Forever.

* * * *

He was fucked. There was no going around that. Any way he looked, every idea he had fell apart like the mist that vanished with the sun.

Ruarc paused in his wandering of the streets and watched the bright streaks of red and orange in the sky. It was a beautiful sunrise. Any other day he might take it as a good omen. But he knew truths now that he hadn't before. Truths that changed *everything*.

The rage inside him threatened to explode. He wanted to hurt something. No. He wanted to tear the limbs from the six individuals who had put him in this tenuous position. There was only one outcome for him. He didn't fear death. He dreaded everything he would leave behind.

Ruarc leaned a shoulder against a building and dropped his head into his hands. Emotion, viscous and cloying, choked him. He might feel better if he could let out a bellow, slam his fist into a wall, or...something. But he couldn't. He was being watched by those who controlled whether his family lived or died. One wrong move, and they could be taken from him. He'd once given up everything for them. How could he let anything happen to his family now?

He lifted his head. Dublin never truly slept. No city did. The dawning of a new day sent the seedier individuals to their holes to await the night while other opportunistic people began to fill the streets. Ruarc didn't know which he found more abhorrent.

Milling among the mortals were Fae—Dark and Light, alike. Some Dark didn't bother to hide their red eyes or their silver-streaked black hair. In this day and age where humans sported various hair colors and eye shades, thanks to contacts, no one paid them any heed. Mortals were unconsciously drawn to Fae. Ruarc rarely walked among humans them without lowering his power so they didn't gather around him. Some Fae got off on having that kind of control over mortals. He never had. He found it a nuisance. It made the humans look weak. No other being reacted to the Fae the way mortals did, and to most Fae who were egomaniacs, it gave them a god-like complex.

Ruarc didn't hate humans. He didn't like them either. They were a part of Earth. Just as the Dragon Kings were. If Ruarc had his preference, he'd be back on the Fae Realm not having to deal with mortals or the Kings.

But he wasn't on the Fae Realm. He was on Earth.

"In fekking Hell," he murmured.

About Donna Grant

New York Times and *USA Today* bestselling author Donna Grant has been praised for her "totally addictive" and "unique and sensual" stories. Her latest acclaimed series, Dragon Kings, features a thrilling combination of dragons, Fae, and immortal Highlanders who are dark, dangerous, and irresistible. She lives with an assortment of animals in Texas.

Visit Donna at:
 www.DonnaGrant.com and
 www.MotherOfDragonsBooks.com

Discover 1001 Dark Nights

COLLECTION FOUR
ROCK CHICK REAWAKENING by Kristen Ashley ~ ADORING
INK by Carrie Ann Ryan ~ SWEET RIVALRY by K. Bromberg ~
SHADE'S LADY by Joanna Wylde ~ RAZR by Larissa Ione ~
ARRANGED by Lexi Blake ~ TANGLED by Rebecca Zanetti ~
HOLD ME by J. Kenner ~ SOMEHOW, SOME WAY by Jennifer
Probst ~ TOO CLOSE TO CALL by Tessa Bailey ~ HUNTED by
Elisabeth Naughton ~ EYES ON YOU by Laura Kaye ~ BLADE by
Alexandra Ivy/Laura Wright ~ DRAGON BURN by Donna Grant ~
TRIPPED OUT by Lorelei James ~ STUD FINDER by Lauren Blakely
~ MIDNIGHT UNLEASHED by Lara Adrian ~ HALLOW BE THE
HAUNT by Heather Graham ~ DIRTY FILTHY FIX by Laurelin Paige
~ THE BED MATE by Kendall Ryan ~ NIGHT GAMES by CD Reiss
~ NO RESERVATIONS by Kristen Proby ~ DAWN OF
SURRENDER by Liliana Hart

COLLECTION FIVE
BLAZE ERUPTING by Rebecca Zanetti ~ ROUGH RIDE by Kristen
Ashley ~ HAWKYN by Larissa Ione ~ RIDE DIRTY by Laura Kaye ~
ROME'S CHANCE by Joanna Wylde ~ THE MARRIAGE
ARRANGEMENT by Jennifer Probst ~ SURRENDER by Elisabeth
Naughton ~ INKED NIGHTS by Carrie Ann Ryan ~ ENVY by Rachel
Van Dyken ~ PROTECTED by Lexi Blake ~ THE PRINCE by Jennifer
L. Armentrout ~ PLEASE ME by J. Kenner ~ WOUND TIGHT by
Lorelei James ~ STRONG by Kylie Scott ~ DRAGON NIGHT by
Donna Grant ~ TEMPTING BROOKE by Kristen Proby ~
HAUNTED BE THE HOLIDAYS by Heather Graham ~ CONTROL
by K. Bromberg ~ HUNKY HEARTBREAKER by Kendall Ryan ~
THE DARKEST CAPTIVE by Gena Showalter

COLLECTION SIX
DRAGON CLAIMED by Donna Grant ~ ASHES TO INK by Carrie
Ann Ryan ~ ENSNARED by Elisabeth Naughton ~ EVERMORE by
Corinne Michaels ~ VENGEANCE by Rebecca Zanetti ~ ELI'S
TRIUMPH by Joanna Wylde ~ CIPHER by Larissa Ione ~ RESCUING
MACIE by Susan Stoker ~ ENCHANTED by Lexi Blake ~ TAKE THE
BRIDE by Carly Phillips ~ INDULGE ME by J. Kenner ~ THE KING
by Jennifer L. Armentrout ~ QUIET MAN by Kristen Ashley ~

ABANDON by Rachel Van Dyken ~ THE OPEN DOOR by Laurelin Paige ~ CLOSER by Kylie Scott ~ SOMETHING JUST LIKE THIS by Jennifer Probst ~ BLOOD NIGHT by Heather Graham ~ TWIST OF FATE by Jill Shalvis ~ MORE THAN PLEASURE YOU by Shayla Black ~ WONDER WITH ME by Kristen Proby ~ THE DARKEST ASSASSIN by Gena Showalter

COLLECTION SEVEN
THE BISHOP by Skye Warren ~ TAKEN WITH YOU by Carrie Ann Ryan ~ DRAGON LOST by Donna Grant ~ SEXY LOVE by Carly Phillips ~ PROVOKE by Rachel Van Dyken ~ RAFE by Sawyer Bennett ~ THE NAUGHTY PRINCESS by Claire Contreras ~ THE GRAVEYARD SHIFT by Darynda Jones ~ CHARMED by Lexi Blake ~ SACRIFICE OF DARKNESS by Alexandra Ivy ~ THE QUEEN by Jen Armentrout ~ BEGIN AGAIN by Jennifer Probst ~ VIXEN by Rebecca Zanetti ~ SLASH by Laurelin Paige ~ THE DEAD HEAT OF SUMMER by Heather Graham ~ WILD FIRE by Kristen Ashley ~ MORE THAN PROTECT YOU by Shayla Black ~ LOVE SONG by Kylie Scott ~ CHERISH ME by J. Kenner ~ SHINE WITH ME by Kristen Proby

COLLECTION EIGHT
DRAGON REVEALED by Donna Grant ~ CAPTURED IN INK by Carrie Ann Ryan ~ SECURING JANE by Susan Stoker ~ WILD WIND by Kristen Ashley ~ DARE TO TEASE by Carly Phillips ~ VAMPIRE by Rebecca Zanetti ~ MAFIA KING by Rachel Van Dyken ~ THE GRAVEDIGGER'S SON by Darynda Jones ~ FINALE by Skye Warren ~ MEMORIES OF YOU by J. Kenner ~ SLAYED BY DARKNESS by Alexandra Ivy ~ TREASURED by Lexi Blake ~ THE DAREDEVIL by Dylan Allen ~ BOND OF DESTINY by Larissa Ione ~ MORE THAN POSSESS YOU by Shayla Black ~ HAUNTED HOUSE by Heather Graham ~ MAN FOR ME by Laurelin Paige ~ THE RHYTHM METHOD by Kylie Scott ~ JONAH BENNETT by Tijan ~ CHANGE WITH ME by Kristen Proby ~ THE DARKEST DESTINY by Gena Showalter

Discover Blue Box Press
TAME ME by J. Kenner ~ TEMPT ME by J. Kenner ~ DAMIEN by J. Kenner ~ TEASE ME by J. Kenner ~ REAPER by Larissa Ione ~ THE

SURRENDER GATE by Christopher Rice ~ SERVICING THE TARGET by Cherise Sinclair ~ THE LAKE OF LEARNING by Steve Berry and M.J. Rose ~ THE MUSEUM OF MYSTERIES by Steve Berry and M.J. Rose ~ TEASE ME by J. Kenner ~ FROM BLOOD AND ASH by Jennifer L. Armentrout ~ QUEEN MOVE by Kennedy Ryan ~ THE HOUSE OF LONG AGO by Steve Berry and M.J. Rose ~ THE BUTTERFLY ROOM by Lucinda Riley ~ A KINGDOM OF FLESH AND FIRE by Jennifer L. Armentrout ~ THE LAST TIARA by M.J. Rose ~ THE CROWN OF GILDED BONES by Jennifer L. Armentrout ~ THE MISSING SISTER by Lucinda Riley ~ THE END OF FOREVER by Steve Berry and M.J. Rose ~ THE STEAL by C. W. Gortner and M.J. Rose ~ CHASING SERENITY by Kristen Ashley ~ A SHADOW IN THE EMBER by Jennifer L. Armentrout

On Behalf of 1001 Dark Nights,

Liz Berry, M.J. Rose, and Jillian Stein would like to thank ~

Steve Berry
Doug Scofield
Benjamin Stein
Kim Guidroz
Social Butterfly PR
Ashley Wells
Asha Hossain
Chris Graham
Chelle Olson
Kasi Alexander
Jessica Saunders
Dylan Stockton
Kate Boggs
Richard Blake
and Simon Lipskar

Made in United States
North Haven, CT
21 January 2022